SOUTH OF SOUTH:

AN ANTHOLOGY DEVOTED TO THE HUMANITY AND NARRATIVE OF MIGRATION

SOUTH OF SOUTH:

AN ANTHOLOGY ON MIGRATION
THE HUMANITY AND NARRATIVE
OF MIGRATION

EDITED BY

NII AYIKWEI PARKES

UNIVERSITY OF
Southampton

PEEPAL TREE

First published in Great Britain in 2011
Peepal Tree Press Ltd
17 King's Avenue
Leeds LS6 1QS
UK

ISBN 13: 9781845231545

This publication was made possible by funding from the
University of Southampton

Supported by
ARTS COUNCIL
ENGLAND

CONTENTS

FOREWORD

Most migrants arrive at their destinations by a combination of serendipity and choicelessness. This has been my experience. The question – *how did you arrive here?* – is always answered with a convoluted mix of myth, love, family ties, budget, language, persecution, opportunity and interruption. In the answer to that question lie the connecting lines of *my* scatter points – Abidjan, Grimsby, Cape Coast, London, Accra, Manchester, Los Angeles, and Dijon. In the answer to that question lie the humanity and narrative of migration – which is the focus of this anthology. So it is pleasing, with hindsight, to find that this anthology – by serendipity of place and time – is interwoven with my tenure as International Writing Fellow at the University of Southampton.

I applied for the position late: an e-mail from Nicky Marsh was forwarded to me by Becky Clarke, who had just edited Monica Arac de Nyeko in the anthology from which her Caine Prize winning story, "The Jambula Tree", was taken. Monica – an intra-African migrant from Uganda to Kenya – would later be one of the first people I invited to contribute to the anthology. Also considering the fellowship was Brian Chikwava, who has also contributed a fine story for the anthology. The other contributors' links to Southampton can be traced by just a couple of steps of association, whether by the water that reaches into the heart of the city as in Dhaka and Chicago, religious ties, or the history of ports shared with Cape Town and New York. However the paths are drawn, this is a rich mix of writing, re-imagining the constantly evolving dynamics of trans-national migration in the 21st century, exploring the complex fabric of the world that contemporary migrants negotiate.

It is only right that the University of Southampton, a centre for the study of postcolonial literatures, diasporas, globalisation, and migration, should take the lead in encouraging the exploration of migration through prose, for Southampton is the city from which the *Mayflower* departed – an event which had huge impact not only on the demographics of the Americas, but also on the ideas of democracy that hold sway in the world today. For this great foresight, I must thank Keiren Phelan and the Arts Council of England for financing the project, and – most importantly – the staff and faculty of the English Department, especially Peter Middleton, Nicky Marsh, Stephen Morton, Sujala Singh, Professor Clare Hanson and Ms Sandy White since without their passion and support this project might never have come to be.

Nii Ayikwei Parkes

NO WORK, NO WATER

TAHMIMA ANAM

Tinku wears an Orange jumpsuit. Around his neck is a string with a tag. The tag says Amer Ali Yussuf. Nabeel Corporation, Dubai, THE WORLD.

Yussuf is Tinku's passport name. From now on he will be known as Yussuf. Afraid he might be summoned in the roll call, he chants the name to himself. He wonders how he should sign his name in the letters home. Of course, he himself will not be signing; he will be paying Awwal 200 taka per page, which is what he charged to fill out Tinku's application to Deshantori Manpower Industries. Awwal's passport name is Mohammad Al-Osama. His name was not Osama before but he wrote Osama on the passport application and proved the magical power of his learning by changing his name. Tinku has got the idea of referring to himself as Yussuf from Awwal-turned-Osama. But that is why they are here, warming themselves by huddling together on the carpet of Dubai airport, because one of their group is named Osama.

Tinku shifts under the blue airport lights. He is jolly; it is the first day he can remember when he has not fallen asleep with the ache of the fields in his feet.

At the barracks Tinku selects his bed. The upper bunks are already full of men who have the satisfied air of knowing where everything is. They dangle their legs over the side of their bunks and say,

Do what the Supervisor tells you.

Don't talk in the workline.

And whatever you do, for fuck's sake, don't touch the women.

They have been told they are building a hotel but Osama says they are building the world. That is why their badges say "Dubai, THE WORLD". The world, Osama says, is a series of islands being built in the shape of the world. An American actress has bought Brazil, and a racing-car driver was given Spain by the Emir of Dubai. All of the good countries are gone –America, Britain, Japan. No one has bought Africa. There is no Bangladesh on the map, only a gap between India and Thailand.

It is cheaper than owning an actual country, Osama says, inhaling. He has taken up smoking and the payment for letters is now two cigarettes per page.

Right now they are on Australia, which has been renamed OQYANA. OQYANA will have the biggest underwater hotel in the world. Tinku hesitates when he is asked to join the line of men lifting the giant panes of glass that will make up the underwater tanks. He is afraid of the sea. His toes wrinkle around the lip of shoreline. The supervisor opens his arms, smiles, and says, *No work, no water.*

The supervisor keeps Tinku's passport locked in a safe in the office. Osama says, in THE WORLD, you will not need a visa to get from one country to another. This is because they are not really countries but RECLAIMED islands. Tinku asks what is a RE-CLAIMED island and Osama says it is a piece of land that is sucked out of the water and the people who suck it out are the people who own it. Each of the islands on OQYANA will not have a separate immigration, but you will need permission to visit someone's island from the person who has sucked out that piece of the world.

Tinku does not ask how anyone can own a piece of the world, because everything Osama has ever said has turned out to be true so he has no reason not to believe him.

Dearest Amma,

As-Salaam-Alaikum. By the grace of Allah I have received my first payment. I send it to you with Barkat, whose contract is finished and he will be returning to Jamalpur this month. It will reach you before Ramzaan.

Everything is going well here in Dubai. Dubai is very beautiful. There are many tall buildings and it is very clean. If you spit on the sidewalk you have to pay the police 200 dirhams. So no one ever spits on the street also if you have to go to the bathroom you can't squat on the street.

Every morning, Tinku gets into his orange jumpsuit. He puts the tag around his neck. Now it says, "Class C labour – OQYANA, the World".

On Fridays Tinku washes the jumpsuit and wears a kurta-pajama and cap to the mosque. In the afternoon he changes into pants and a red shirt. In the evening he wears his lungi and sits at his desk and recites the Arabic alphabet.

He is starting to understand a few snatches of Arabic. He takes pleasure in deciphering the opening lines of the Qur'an. He waits for a letter from his mother. He watches Osama's teeth redden from the cigarettes; his own arms grow black and muscular. He stops wondering if it will ever rain. In the spring, cooled by the electric fan he has bought with his wages, he listens to Osama read that his mother has died. The money he has sent has paid for the burial and the Qul-Khani. The guests were fed samosas and sweets.

His sister has gone to live with their grandmother in a neighbouring village. She writes to say she wants to get married. She asks him to send a gold set.

Tinku wants to marry too. He has been saving money for a set for his bride, but he sends the money to his sister. In return he gets a photo of his sister in front of a snowcapped mountain. Standing stiffly beside his sister is a man in a brown suit. He has pulled the sleeve up to reveal a wristwatch. His sister looks worried, but very pretty in a magenta sari and matching slippers. Tinku pastes the photo to the wall beside his bunk, whispering to her that she should be obedient, faithful, and bear sons.

Because they work in shifts and because they have lights bright enough to turn night into day, the world's largest underwater hotel is built in under two years. By this time, Tinku is no longer afraid of the sea. He has pressed his cheek against the blue and watched the weeds sway and the fish burst into view. He has seen a dozen stingrays and even a small shark on the other side of the glass. The supervisor has said these sharks do not bite. If the Arabian Sea had biting sharks, nobody would buy the islands of The World.

On his very last day, Tinku packs his electric fan, his colour television set, and his Qur'an. He wears a brown suit like his brother-in-law. This time, at the airport, he can read the signs in Arabic. He joins the queue for foreign nationals. He thumbs his green passport, which was returned to him that morning. When the official asks his name, he says, without hesitation, Amer Ali Yussuf.

THE ROVER

ROMESH GUNESEKERA

Colin Mahalingam had assumed that a mustard-yellow Rover would give him some status on the streets of Manila; he was wrong. English cars did not cut much ice, except for the Finance Minister's Rolls. He braked and turned, missing by about a centimetre – another meaningless unit, like grams and kilos, for a man brought up on imperial measures – a flamboyant jeepney crammed with school girls. "Oi vey," he exclaimed to himself, not knowing quite why. He was not Jewish, nor was he a bad driver. He was not a fast one either, and Ayala Avenue was busy this Friday afternoon with jeepneys, buses, vans and cars of all persuasions.

He'd left the office earlier than usual because he had finished his piece for the Far East's newest business bulletin a day early. Not by plan, but by chance: Mr Diliman was in town for only two days and he had granted Colin his interview on Wednesday. Colin had a clear day to write up the piece and he had found no good reason for putting it off. He managed to add in a bit about the Muslim south which he reckoned would please his boss, Solomon. For the first time in ages he had a Friday afternoon in which he could clear his desk and ignore the ten p.m. deadline. He had handed in his copy to Emily, the new sub, and now was ready for a bucket of balls at the driving range and a long cool sundowner with his buddy, Carlos. His golf was about on par with his driving, but it did give him more of a sense of achievement. Although he was prone to slices and hooks – balls going everywhere except straight – it didn't cause him too much

13

anguish. He was happy enough to be able to hit the ball and remembered only too well how often he used to miss everything and pirouette in the air like a circus dolphin when he had first started playing the game. Colin was not a natural golfer. Back in Ceylon he had steered clear of the golf club – that was not his milieu. He did his drinking at the rugger club where the beer was cheaper and the bar more geared to non-players. When he had come to Manila – six months ago, in the wake of the debacle of the Beatles one-night stand and disastrous local press – he found himself with more privileges, as a foreigner, than he had expected to find anywhere. He ate at more expensive restaurants, drank at fancier night clubs, and seemed on the whole to have gone upmarket in his lifestyle. The Polo Club was not within his reach but many of the golf clubs that were, were very swish.

"You are a lucky fellow, Colin," Solomon had said when he'd started at the magazine. "You did the right thing to come here. If in doubt always head east."

"From anywhere?"

"Asia is awakening, Colin. Where would you be if you had gone west?"

"You mean to England?"

Solomon nodded. "You know what has happened to Nando? He went to London. Fleet Street. Ha, no chance. Bugger is writing annual reports in a Bayswater basement shit creek. Go west, you go down. Go east, you go up. Look at what the British did, the French, the whole lot. Eastward, go!"

Colin cocked his head and let his boss's wisdom collect in a little puddle. Luck, he had to admit, was on his side. The newspaper he worked for in Colombo had been mired in politics during the general election the previous year. He was not only fed up with the paper, he was in trouble with the editor, the proprietor and the two opposing political parties that swapped power from election to election; he had to get out fast. Solomon's number two, Palitha, had been one of his batch mates and told him about the agency they'd set up in Manila. There was a job there that was his for the asking. Colin was not usually a man of quick decisions; he preferred the pace of weeklies, even monthlies. After a night of beer and buriyani, with a couple of drunken

14

hacks, he had made his decision and took a plane to Singapore and then to Manila, leaving behind everything except a suitcase of books and his portable typewriter.

★

The driving range was about ten minutes drive down the highway under normal circumstances, but Colin stayed in the slow lane and took his time. About half a kilometre before he needed to, he flicked his indicator; he tried to concentrate on the road the way he did with his new Gary Player driver: he wiggled the steering wheel to straighten the car as he would the wooden club-head to bring it close to the teed-up ball and order the world. The car shuddered. The Diliman piece had left him peculiarly unsatis-fied. There was something that did not make sense in the story, but he couldn't work out what it was. Diliman had claimed that two years ago, in 1965, when Ferdinand Marcos – the future President – had come to his Association of Passion Fruit Growers annual conference, he had promised a fruit juice vending contract that would cover all government offices in return for the Associa-tion's cash for his election campaign. A fair enough deal in the business of politics and ripe for reneging in the normal jumble of democratic barter. But Diliman was not happy with the way things had turned out. In his interview with Colin he had pulled at his flabby cheeks thoughtfully and said, "I don' think we can trust this President."

Colin sighed as he shifted down a gear. He had decided not to use the quote. On a newspaper you learn to trust very little, except your instincts, and his instincts told him to keep the politicians out of the story for the moment. He found it quite liberating.

He took the turn off the highway with a sense of elation. Perhaps it was the soft suspension on the left that gave him the lift. Frank Marston, the First Secretary at the British Embassy, who had sold him the car had said it was a design feature of this particular model. "Very useful," he'd added. "She is as good as any American limo in riding the sleeping policemen on these roads, but tight as a belt around the bend, if you know what I mean?" Colin didn't think he had fully tested the limits of the car, but the knowledge of its fundamental qualities comforted him. Oddly enough, he trusted Frank. The knotted accent in which he spoke as he tried to modify his English with pips and squeaks to the Pilipino-American around him, was something that allayed Colin's own anxieties. The fact that it was a right-hand drive in a left-hand country did not trouble him at the time.

The road to the golf club went past a small new executive *barrio* of expensive housing around an artificial lake – the brainchild of a young entrepreneur from La Union. Colin's golf buddy, Carlos, lived in the newest of these. He was an architect who literally inhabited his creations, learning from each how to improve on the next. He was never in the same place for more than nine months. His golf was on a level with Colin's and they liked to play together because they kept pace with each other as two carts might on a winding road. At the driving range they always reached the end of their buckets – 90 balls – within minutes of each other.

The trees on the main road were in flower; the tiny red blossom pricking the wavering blue blur of the afternoon sky seeming to make the slow rolling clouds thicken at the edges. There could be rain in them, collecting in the dark bruises on the low swollen undersides, but Colin reckoned it wouldn't break through before dark and that he should be able to whack a bucketful before the downpour. He rolled down a window to test the air. It was dry enough. He could smell wood smoke and burnt sesame oil wafting across the quiet side-streets named after various random species of fish: Mullet Lane, Barracuda Avenue, Marlin Drive. His friend Carlos had explained that the developer was a keen angler; he'd called the village Fisherman's Cove – a retreat from Manila – although it was nowhere near the sea. The ads for the residences were real angler's tales, he'd laughed. Fantasy...

The entrance to the golf club had a barrier controlled by a security guard armed with a machine gun. He recognized Colin and raised the pole. Colin stopped the car under it. "Hey, Pedro, you use that gun yet?"

The guard smiled. "Only three bullets, sir. For emergency."

"Helluva machine gun," Colin said.

"Yes, sir." The guard patted the gun. "Good only for little rabbit."

The driving range was located to the left of the main clubhouse. It had its own bar and service centre. Colin noticed his friend's car – Carlos had a blue convertible – parked in its usual place. He pulled in next to it. He switched off the engine but didn't get out immediately. A local garage had fitted the air conditioner in the staid Rover and it seemed very awkwardly placed. Condensation dripped out of it onto his trouser leg, always marking him with an embarrassing damp patch after a drive. He had tried taping plastic to the box, but it never stayed stuck. It was a car of many minor trials, but he had grown fond of it.

The smack and wallop of clubs against balls ran up and down the bays in a slow random pattern. He reckoned the place was not too full; most people would turn up about an hour later. Carlos would be at the bar, he never liked to play on his own – even to practice alone at the driving range.

Colin collected his clubs from the back of the car and made his way to the terrace. Carlos raised his glass. "Hey, Colin. Calamansi?"

Colin nodded. Juice now, booze later. "Plenty of room out there?"

"No problem. No one down on the left."

"Bay number 30?"

"Yup. You can slice your shots as much as you like down there."

Colin looked at him sharply, but his friend was not mocking him; he was simply optimising space as he was so expensively trained to do. Carlos had watery eyes and the face of a inebriated cherub at any time of the day and whatever he was drinking: tea, juice or rum. Although only in his early forties, he had travelled to many parts of the world, before settling into his niche in Manila's booming business of bespoke property development. His talent was in creating small countries out of his houses, using the cultural traditions of Indonesia, or Thailand, or Spain, or Greece to evoke the ambience of living in one of them. "A culture trip," he would say. A fantasy oasis for wealthy businessmen who liked to trace their origins, or their pleasures, to exotic locations from Bangkok to Bath. "I pick the place out of a kids' book – *The Child's Guide to the Countries of the World*. I hated my geography teacher, but I loved that book. I have a system for picking a number and that gives me a new page every time." When Colin had looked puzzled he had explained, "Otherwise I will think of the same number, or try to go for somewhere specific in the alphabet, you know. You have to trick the subconscious. Otherwise it is no good." Space in the mind, fantasy furniture. Colin understood. His subconscious too needed a great deal of tricking whenever he sat at his typewriter.

On this day though, as he unslung his golf bag and stood it on the floor next to the cane chair opposite Carlos, his subconscious slipped a gear all on its own and brought up an image that frightened him. He saw a corpse, face down in a puddle, on a concrete drive. He closed his eyes for a second to turn over the body; he recognized the face as Diliman's.

"What's wrong, Colin. Sit down a minute." Carlos pushed out a chair.

Colin took a big breath of air and leant on the chair. "He is a dead man."

"Sure," Carlos said. "In the long run we all are. Have a drink. You talking about your boss?"

Colin shook his head. "I met Diliman, you know, the fruit juice king creep. Big interview. But just now I saw his body."

Carlos's eyes widened. His broad face grew broader. "Here? Dead at the club."

"Just an image flashed through my mind."

"Wishful thinking, my friend. Just wishful."

Colin shrugged. Diliman was nothing more than this week's interview subject as far as he was concerned: wallpaper for eight-hundred words in the middle-page slot. A fruit magnate held no particular charm for him. He knew many people would have liked Diliman squashed – fruit was a big and lethal business in this country – but Colin was not one of them. He wished no harm to the man. He had had one premonition in his life and that was eight years ago. The night before SWRD, the Prime Minister of Ceylon, was assassinated Colin had been drinking with his usual crowd at the rugger club. Someone had started a game of *Who am I*? Colin had pretended to be the Prime Minister and one of his friends, Siva, had chosen to be the vicar of the local Anglican church. That night Colin had dreamed that the vicar had abandoned the church for the temple and the Prime Minister had exchanged his pen for a sword. There had been an argument at the end of which the Prime Minister was found dead. The next day SWRD was killed by Somarama, an enraged Buddhist monk. Colin never told anyone about the dream; it had frightened him too much. Not that he felt responsible in any way; only that he felt uncertain and used.

"I have nothing against him. But I guess he seemed a little funny..."

"A clown?"

"Do you think people know when something is going to happen?"

Carlos scratched at his ear. "Colin, what are you thinking? You think you know what's going to happen? Let's go to the races then and place a fucking bet. What the hell are we doing here at a golf club?"

"No, I mean I thought he might have sensed something."

"Oh, oh. So he knows he is going to die?"

"Maybe he doesn't, but some part of him does. Like his subconscious. Maybe it gives off signals. Makes him think of things. He acted as though he suspected something."

"Like maybe that he was talking to a madman? Come on, Colin, let's go bash a few balls." Carlos finished his drink and stood up. They ambled over to the bays at the far end. Carlos had already put his bag in number 30 and two buckets of balls. "I got you a bucket," he said to Colin. "I want to hit that board today."

"The 250 yard marker?"

Carlos nodded and picked up his driver. "Yup."

★

Carlos never hit his target that day. He didn't even quite get to the 200 yard marker, which Colin managed. It was a solace to him – not just the length of his drive, but the unit of its measurement. Thank God for golf, he thought as he slipped the covers on his clubs. What could one do with metres?

"Beer?" He offered Carlos as consolation.

While they were waiting for the beer, Frank Marston turned up. He nodded at Colin, "Good Evening."

Carlos looked flummoxed and checked his watch. Colin said, "Oh, hello." Then he introduced the two men to each other.

"You are from England?" Carlos asked.

Frank Marston gave a nervous little laugh. "Yes, how did you know?"

"Wild guess."

"Frank is the guy I bought my car from," Colin added.

"Right. The British car?"

"Going all right, I hope."

Colin nodded happily. "Yes. Yes, it goes very smoothly."

"What you drive now?" Carlos asked looking over at the parking lot.

"A Lincoln. I am afraid I have given in to the Americans. In the end we all seem to..."

"Nice move." Carlos smiled.

★

When Colin had visited Frank Marston at his house in Bel Air to pick up the yellow Rover, he had been surprised. Although from the outside it was not particularly different from any of the other lavish Bel Air residences – manicured lawn, tailored bushes, clean white paint, shutters and decorative iron bars on the windows – when he stepped through the front door, he felt transported into a familiar but misplaced world. The smell of turmeric, coriander and fenugreek hung in the afternoon air – unusual in a Manila home where the aftermath of lunch tended to be sweeter and dryer, fishier, if not simply American. The wood furniture in the open plan room was dark and heavy and highly wrought; there were divans with block-printed cotton cushions, several woven rugs with elaborate Indian designs, a large statue of Ganesh on a tall marble column guarding a corridor leading to the rest of the house.

Frank Marston had appeared, extending his hand. "Hello, Colin. I am sorry, I was having a nap. It is so hot these days."

Colin was a good journalist. He never showed surprise however unexpected things might be. Frank Marston's crumpled kurta and pajamas, his tan chappals, the tousled hair he had taken

20

in without even blinking. "I am sorry if I am too early, but the journey was shorter than I expected. Taxis these days go very fast."

"Not to worry. Glad you are here. A cup of tea?"

Colin had nodded. The tea, he reckoned, was likely to be good and a rare treat outside his own home. "With milk?"

"Of course. Proper tea, here. But Indian, you understand?" He had called the maid and instructed her in careful English.

"It feels very Indian, your house," Colin had said with a nod at Ganesh.

"Sit down, please sit down." Frank had gestured at one of the large chairs. "I was in New Delhi for five years before coming to Manila. A big change, as no doubt you have found too."

"You must be very fond of India."

Frank had smiled. "Yes, you could say that. I had an Ambassador there I loved."

"Oh, really?" This time, Colin had been taken aback.

"I couldn't really bring her over with me. It was not... Practical."

"I can imagine," Colin had said, although he could not quite. He had thought he understood powerful men – he'd interviewed enough of them – but he would never have classed Frank Marston as one. The Frank he had met for the first time at the golf club had been a shy and tentative sort of person. They had started talking only because they had double-booked a game and it seemed easier to pair up than wait for another slot on a busy Sunday morning. It took until the fourth hole – a par five with three treacherous water hazards in which they both lost two balls – for a conversation to develop. They had played one other game together during which the sale of the Rover had come up and Colin had decided to go for it precisely because Frank seemed a quiet, unassuming and honest chap.

"The Rover belonged to my predecessor and I thought it had a sort of affinity, you might say, to my old car."

"I see." Colin had nodded.

"But it is not quite the same thing. There is nothing wrong with the car, you understand. Nothing at all, but it is not quite the same as the old thing. Perhaps you can't hang on to past... affections. I think a complete change is in order for me." He had looked around the large room with its frosted louvres and mosquito mesh. "One has to make one's adjustments incrementally, don't you think? It takes a little while to feel at home in a new place."

The tea had come, and after he had had a sip, Colin had tried to clarify matters. "The Ambassador in India..." he had started.

"You mean the High Commissioner, or do you mean my car?"

"Car?"

"It would never do here. It needs a driver who understands it. It is a very symbiotic creature – the Ambassador. You don't have these Indian cars in Ceylon, do you?"

Colin had taken a deep breath and adjusted things in his mind. "No we don't, but we do have Rovers. At least of a certain vintage."

"There you are. Perfect for you here then. You will feel quite at home sitting in it."

★

Now, Colin felt the need to make another set of minor adjustments. He noticed that Frank was indeed looking more American. His golfing pants, the polo shirt, the cap in his hands were all American; there was nothing English, nor Indian, about him, except when he spoke.

"You know, Carlos, you should see Frank's house. You will appreciate it. He has a real sense of India in his house: furniture, rugs, everything."

"Really? India?"

"He lived in India before coming to Manila."

"Cool."

"Carlos is an architect," Colin said to Frank. "He designs houses to create exactly your kind of atmosphere."

Frank looked quite cool. "What are you working on?"

"Balinese house. I wish I could do India, but I've never done it."

"There are many different Indias."

"Yeah?"

"North, south. Moghul. Hindu."

22

"Philippines too. We have many Philippines. Have you been south?"

Colin felt a cold shadow on him. The geography was unfamiliar; it was too much for him. He had left Ceylon in a hurry. He hadn't even brought a packet of tea with him, let alone an almirah or a car. Even his memories were suspect: jostled and jumbled. He could write a story – that was all. A story of the here and now, the living. Business and businessmen with the occasional flash of subconscious wit. He couldn't speak Tagalog, but he could speak English. His mother tongue was a noise that made no sense to anyone in the neighbourhood he now lived in. Geography did that without his noticing it. He thought Frank, almost a chameleon it seemed, might be someone he'd like to know better.

"Frank, would you like to join us for dinner after your golf. We go over to Mario's in Makati. You'd be very welcome. They have burgers as well as adobo."

Frank looked startled. "Dinner?"

"Yeah, come and join us," Carlos added.

Frank's eyes switched from Colin to Carlos and back again. "I wouldn't want to intrude."

"Come on, Frank. I want to know all about India," Carlos urged.

★

The restaurant had been built to look like a Spanish galleon. There were two upper terraces that served cocktails and bar snacks between anchors and rigging, a middle lower deck that was designed for al fresco dining and two cabins for those who preferred the comfort of air-conditioned sherry casks.

The three of them drove up in their separate vehicles and parked alongside each other: the Rover first, then the longer convertible and lastly the large Lincoln. Carlos was a natural host and took the lead. "Come, come, Frank," he said. "You like to be inside or out?"

"Out is fine. I imagine you prefer it too," he nodded at Carlos's convertible.

23

"Ha, ha," his laugh always seemed artificial to Colin, but was never forced. "Like my car?"

"Yes."

They took a table by the traveller's palm. A waitress in a grass skirt brought them a tray of Mario's signature cocktails. "Complimentary, sir."

"These are the best in the world," Carlos said. "*Mabuhay*, Frank. Good to meet you."

"Cheers," Frank replied. "Very good. Rum, I suppose."

Carlos winked. "Right."

"And passion fruit, I believe," Colin added with a private smile.

"They like rum in England?" Carlos asked, settling back in his chair and crossing his legs expansively. His foot waggled as he sipped.

"Not so popular as here. Not in India either."

"Shame. But that's why you have to come here to the Philippines. Every hour is happy hour. How long you been in Manila, Frank? You like it?"

"I like it a lot. It is about eighteen months now. I am half way through my posting, but I am only just beginning to find my way."

"Like Colin. All still new, hey. That's good. New is good. I change my house every year to get that new perspective, you know. See afresh. Very important in this life."

Colin always tried to see things afresh too; if you were going to be a good journalist you had to be able to do that. You had to understand what was really going on. Keen, sharp eyes. A subconscious that did not interfere. No baggage. He looked at Frank and felt a little confused. All that baggage, but picked up from nowhere. Why New Delhi? He flicked open the menu. Usually at Mario's he would always have the grilled chicken, but today he thought he might try beef for the first time in his life. A burger, or a T-bone steak even. Religious habits were hard to shake, he thought, but this might be the day… As he ran his finger down the options, he felt Frank's eyes on him. I am living in Manila, he thought to himself. A new country. A new world.

Then, as the waitress approached with her order-pad and

pencil, a volley of gunshots rang out. Someone screamed from the front of the restaurant and a car roared off.

"Not another fucking shoot out." Carlos gulped back his drink.

The whole place had gone silent. Colin's finger hovered in mid-air. Then he put the menu down. "I'm going to go see what happened?"

"You wanna be a reporter now?"

"Perhaps you should wait, don't you think?" Frank added.

The restaurant was seeping back into life as Colin made his way to the front. The deck manager mumbled a string of incoherent apologies. Outside, the parking lot glittered with broken glass. The doorman held him back. "Sorry, sir. Bad thing, sir. Your car…"

By his Rover lay two crumpled bodies. He recognized Bunny Diliman despite the blood smearing his face. Three bullet holes had punctured the side of his Rover. The windows were smashed. A couple of security guards were wandering about in a daze. On the main street the traffic flowed unperturbed: jeepneys, buses, big American cars. He thought he heard a siren. He checked his watch. "I need the telephone," he said to the manager who had come to his side.

He called Solomon, his boss, who liked to fiddle with the pages until the last minute, every Friday night with the fresh and eager Emily in his teak-lined office. "It'll have to be an obituary," Colin said. "You'll need this as a new first para." He dictated five sentences with his eyes closed, giving the plain facts and the merest hint of a premonition.

RAISING THE TONE

ZOË WICOMB

Miriam yawns, stretches, and chucks her pencil across the table. Boring, boring, boring.

Then, remembering Babylon, she leaps on to the bed, arms flung out dramatically, and mimics, stuttering aloud, I am a B – b – british object, before collapsing and burying her face in the pillow. What a fine start that is to a story, and with so many examples of fine stories in the world, why, oh why can *she* not get started. Even her own story would do. Everyone should be able to think herself as the subject of a narrative, and with a trumpeting opening line like that. Except, it should be revised at the beginning of every year, otherwise people would end up like her mother – stuck in history. And a concrete pipe springs to mind, with half the old girl's body, her torso, wriggled free, but alas, the full hips unable to move any further. Stuck. Thus, unable to think herself into a different story, it is always the same opening line, and *in medias res*, since she knows that everyone she knows, knows her story, which, far from causing embarrassment, seems to bring comfort. That's the problem with grown-ups, updating their stories ever more infrequently, until they clean forget to do so as the mortgage and shopping and clipping of garden hedges take precedence.

Miriam picks up the shopping list that Cath has slipped under her door. Everything about her mother is irritating, just look at that handwriting – pathetic, like a child's. Even a shopping list can't escape the palimpsest of the old story of Africa: walking barefoot the five miles to school: and the well-worn keywords of mieliepap, velskoen, sjambok, police dogs… etcetera, etcetera. If only Miriam could move out today; it wouldn't take more than an hour to fling her few things in a bag. But first things first, a poignant opening line is all she asks for.

No need to write down these, the only words that spring to mind: I am the subject of history. So disappointing – she could flagellate herself – so transparently a product of her class in Postcolonial Writing, which she took only because of her mother's pleading. However, let it now be known that all that compliance is a thing of the past. No wonder she can't squeeze out as much as a decent opening line. The time has come for taking control of her life, of her own education. Overrated, that's what Princess Anne had to say about a university education, and while Miriam hates the idea of sharing a view with such a person, she has to agree. In fact, she can do better, for unlike the princess she has the experience of two years under her belt. University stifles creativity, and in that sense it is underrated. People like her mother think of it as an escalator to the middle classes, a means of blending in (although to *what* is never voiced), the passport to better paid jobs; they fail to appreciate its more subtle functions of knocking the stuffing out of eager youth through the ventriloquy of writing essays, the deadening effect of deadlines and timetables – all in the interest of a stable, unchallenged society, of youth drilled into submission. Not for Miriam, thank you very much; she will not be going back to finish the degree. It may well take time to throw off the bad habits of two long years, but then, who knows what she'd come up with, for sure as eggs is eggs she plans to come up with something original, something startling and creative.

Sure as eggs? Steering a shopping trolley, Miriam has just come to the end of the aisle of biscuits and crap cakes, and there, directly before her is the stand of eggs, an omen to seal her resolve. Lidl is pretty good as far as supermarkets go. The Third World shop, Mrs Dalhousie called it when it first opened, by which she meant that it is overrun with immigrants – Eastern European gypsies, Zimbabwean asylum seekers and such – whilst she hastily added that she doesn't mean anything by that. Then Miriam said that it must have been such a person who, only a month ago, at one of the Sighthill tower blocks, had been killed by his good neighbours, fellow Lidl shoppers, but the woman brushed it aside.

Och, there's no difference between folk the world over, AnnMarie Dalhousie, who had never set foot outside Glasgow claimed, except, there's no point in being careless: in Lidl you do have to keep a close eye on your handbag.

You'd swear the woman's had a university education. Well, Miriam doesn't have a handbag; instead, her mother's purse lies at the bottom of her hessian bag, and that's another good thing about Lidl – no plastic bags wantonly supplied. She grabs the eggs and heads off for the treasure trove of the central aisle full of crazy, unexpected things like riding crops, sewing kits, floral Wellington boots, mosquito nets, stuff for DIY men on the other side, and today a selection of fruit trees. Where on earth would the inhabitants of high-rise flats plant them? Nectarines, surely, would refuse to grow on the banks of the Clyde. On the other hand, these days the car park has a number of four-by-fours, the well-heeled feeling the pinch and descending from their own middle class ghettoes ever since *The Guardian* article that praised Lidl's low prices, organic vegetables, and fancy continental foods. Mrs Dalhousie will be pleased; she is keen on the notion of raising the social tone.

Last week Cath came back with a potted mesembryanthemum, and sickening it was to see her mother hunched over a succulent with fat greyish fingers for leaves and flowers in day-glo pink. Her cheeks were flushed with nostalgia.

All the way from Namaqualand these must have come, she wailed, yes wailed. Who knows how it'll do here.

I thought Namaqualand was dull and dry, semi-desert, with sandstorms that sting your poor bare legs, Miriam mocked. Her mother's stories never quite added up.

Oh, but then the daisies – vygies, that's what we call them – arrive in spring, miraculously covering the veld. Anyway, I would never have described it as dull, she added.

Well, I heard that they're cultivated in a greenhouse just outside Greenock, Miriam lied. So the plant's bound to die out here in the cold, and anyway it hardly looks like a daisy.

She thought it necessary, healthy, to bring her mother back to earth. And the flowers certainly looked frightened, the petals huddled into a protective spear, as if they were still stuck in a travelling crate, or had to retreat under the superior gaze of native plants.

But there was no denting Cath's delight. Not at all, she explained, that's why they're called mesembryanthemum, Greek for the opening of flowers at noon. Greek, you know, that's what we Griquas speak, and she giggled in her high-pitched voice that Miriam has come to label African.

For all this sentimental nonsense the succulent at least was better than the dreadful flowers made out of coloured telephone wire that Cath brings back from home, as she still calls the Cape. Their flat is cluttered with ethnic artefacts – the rubbish drawings in felt-tip pen, rusting little bicycles and carts made out of wire, weird things with bottle tops, corks and bits of glass that her mother loves, and beadwork everywhere. Why would anyone want to cover a gourd with beads? Christ, did those people not learn anything from history? From the exchange of beads and buttons for land? It's enough to make you want to shoot them all over again.

So, why do you want to leave home, Miriam? To that question she could truthfully answer that she's been driven out by beadwork.

Other than a job-lot of Greek foods nearing their sell-by date and indeterminate kids' stuff, there is nothing unusual in the central aisle today. Miriam imagines that there is a Mr Lidl, well, more likely a natty Mr Rab Liddell who, after years of bargaining, still brims with enthusiasm for shopping. On the crack of dawn, Easyjet flights to Berlin, Amsterdam, or Stockholm to pick over the bargains for turning his shop into a bazaar, a real market where, midst the Babel of voices, the old and young, Brits and immigrants alike can pore over the unexpected, marvel at the exotica. Here the local old biddies dragging tartan shopping trollies will nudge a black woman in a towering headdress, or a blonde girl who turns out to speak with a heavy accent: Say hen, what do you make of this? Or, holding up a knobbly celeriac: how do you eat them things? Miriam loves Lidl for being the very opposite of university; this is where she belongs, amongst ordinary people struggling to make ends meet, who delight in the cheap merchandise, even if they struggle with the new, with the weekly challenges posed by Mr Lidl, whose contempt for Tesco is palpable in the very layout of these aisles.

For all her mother's revolutionary credentials, they live in the liminal zone where their modest tenements butt on to fancy town-house terraces on the eastern side, whilst on the west, just over the road, is the working-class estate where six high-rise blocks lean precariously against grey skies. The tenements aspire to the middle-class condition of the terraces. It makes Miriam sick: middle of the road, cautious and quiet, fearful of attention and equally fearful of being overlooked, sitting tight in the middle lane of the motorway, hesitating, hedging their bets, fearful of being called upon to declare themselves, of declaring their opening sentences. People like Mrs Dalhousie (Please call me AnnMarie? Like hell she will) out of whose painted mouth came words like Pakis, gypsies, Jewesses, and them asylum seekers who swamp the high rise where she lives. Not decent folk like youse who speak proper, she said on meeting Miriam's mother a year or more ago. Surely Cath must know that before she had been heard speaking proper, she too was one of those darkies against whom the beleaguered natives must protect their handbags. Does her mother have no pride?

Miriam keeps out of the woman's way, rushes past the living room where Dalhousie is even allowed to smoke, and where, not so long ago she overheard the old bag consoling herself that things are looking up, that new people are raising the tone in the Burnside flats. Miriam can only assume that their car park must be boasting a couple of four-by-fours. But Cath, who these days seems to have lost her marbles, says that AnnMarie has a heart of gold. They are thick as thieves, and Miriam has recently heard her mother come in at six in the morning, which has something to do with Dalhousie, she has let on. But Miriam makes a point of not asking any questions. She keeps out of their way; they disgust her.

Cath teaches a class in childcare at the community centre where AnnMarie brings the grandchild that had been dumped on her. The child is an overgrown, bald, lard-coloured baby whose tiny features squat timidly in the centre of a fat face that grows directly out of its chest and spills over either side of an expensive pram, but Miriam is not allowed to say that. Angel child, her mother calls it.

See how that baby's transformed AnnMarie's life, has brought her close to the other people in the flats. Really, the wee sweetheart has broadened her world, made her see things quite differently.

Well, don't imagine that I'll baby sit for Mrs Raise-the-tone, Miriam warned, but Cath was sniffy. Oh, no need for that at all. AnnMarie's got an amazing system in place, across all the blocks on the estate. Those people are on the ball, really well organised.

For hours, Miriam sits at the table overlooking the street. Now that she's resolved not to return to uni, she really must try harder. But her page as usual is blank. The only progress she has made today is to prevent herself from doodling in the margins. If no words, then neither squiggles, nor any movement: that's her new motto. Which means that her eyes are fixed on the tenements over the road, since being stuck here at the table gives her licence to stare across at the matching first floor flat into the neighbours' rooms. She may not know the MacFarlanes, but she certainly knows their habits: the couple's silent breakfasts in the mornings; the ritual watering of window boxes before they go off to work, in spite of the daily summer rain; the man's return at five thirty when he walks about swigging from a beer bottle. At night Miriam can follow through a lit bathroom window the silhouette of the woman lowering herself on to the toilet. Such sad faith in frosted glass, or do the MacFarlanes know that they can be seen? Miriam is transfixed by the shape shifting, the bent form of elbows resting on thighs until the woman rises, with a sigh perhaps? Twisting into her pants and turning to fasten a zip. Then there is the man, who turns his back, jiggles his shoulders, bends slightly to unzip, and Miriam watches as he finishes, straightens up, and adjusts his clothes. Sure as eggs, there'll be piss on the floor, a drop or two on the seat – that's what men do, even as guests in other people's houses, as if they have never been told that such a poor design requires scrutiny after the act. Thank God there are no men in their house. The very thought makes her gag.

Miriam is nearly nineteen and sick to death of life. Christ, she could so easily take a razor to her throat. Searing pain, how much better that than this steady dum-dum-dum that passes for a heartbeat, this dreary, stultifying, stifling, boring, boring, boring...

Cath is only mildly alarmed. You'll regret it, she says.

It obviously won't be easy to top myself; there wouldn't be any point, would there, if it were easy, but what I really can't do is regret it afterwards. There won't be a me, a sentient subject, I mean a sentient being, to feel regret.

Cath sighs. She means leaving university before finishing the degree, rather than nonsense about topping herself.

Well, that too takes courage, Miriam says. What she yearns for is to take control of her own life, but she has been through this conversation before and with no new arguments, no new entailments, she would rather not go into all that again. Best to avoid repetition, the mouldy story of her mother's years in The Struggle, the predictable lament: Where I come from children respect their elders, appreciate their parents' efforts, not the cheeky, pampered creatures... But Cath too seems to have lost interest. She sits on the sofa staring distractedly at the beaded Zulu blanket; her dejection appears to have nothing to do with their argument, so that Miriam asks, What's up? Without taking her eyes off the blanket, her mother says mildly, flicking her wrist, Oh, off you go. Nothing you'd be interested in, nothing you wouldn't call the old African story.

Dismissed like a kid. Miriam walks straight out the front door without picking up her keys. It is mild, and a walk might do her good, might clear her head for writing. She crosses the main road to the estate of high rise flats where the grounds are inviting, generously landscaped into sweeping hillocks and mini vales, with clumps of mature trees that turn it into something of a park. She might even write something set in that park. Ahead there is a playground with swings and slides and roundabouts where a group of women in salwar kameezes stand gathered around shrieking children. If she keeps away from the playground there should be no danger of running into anyone she knows.

The lawns have just been mown, and the sweet smell of cut grass goes some way towards making up for the dilapidated buildings, incongruous in that lovely setting. Then the sun comes bursting out. Light bounces off gilded window panes so that it is difficult to count the floors, but Miriam does so twice, until she is sure that there are eighteen. Testament to the utopian vision of the sixties, the tower blocks, built for shipyard workers she supposes, stand at various angles to each other, once proud in the landscaped grounds. They all have names, conjuring up the Scottish romance of lochs and mountains, but a number of the letters have fallen off, so that it is a matter of guessing. According to AnnMarie's old story it was bionic, bouffant-headed Thatcher who in the eighties, with no voters in Glasgow, took revenge by killing off shipbuilding. So the original workers packed their bags and left in droves, hence the asylum seekers who are bussed into places like these, pegged into estates where natives have left holes.

Miriam is blinded by forked spears of light from a glass panel, a Blakean moment that announces her future. This is where she should live, in a cheap, council flat. If there is room for immigrants, why not a little flat for her? It would be amazing on the top floor where you'd have a magnificent view of the city. If it were not a Sunday, she would go to the Housing Office right now to check out the possibility. In the meantime, she will nose about the nearest block, perhaps take the lift to the top floor.

At the base of the tower named LO–ON– each steel-rimmed panel below the ground floor windows is entirely covered with paintings. These are clearly the works of foreigners: stylized landscapes with weird flora; seascapes with strange oriental-looking boats; an exotic black woman whose elaborate headdress has taken over, expanded into abstract patterns that fill the entire frame; a copy of one of Hokusai's Mount Fuji views. In each the handling of paint is different. Miriam lingers before the ones that look like frescoes, where the pigment seems to have seeped into the concrete. The same painter, she imagines. How on earth had the artist managed to make his mark in the very fabric of the building? A bold gesture, speaking as much as longing for another place, as inserting himself here in Glasgow into the history of LO–ON–. Her head fizzes with excitement. This is a place where people are alive, where new things are thought and done, where she could get involved.

When a man in green overalls comes through the double doors, she slips in and hurriedly makes for the lift. A group of people follow her; a pale, ginger-haired family of parents and four children crowd into the lift. The children press up against her, and the smell of alcohol and pee makes her stomach heave. The woman, who has no top teeth, says something that Miriam doesn't understand, but she nods her head vigorously and smiles. As they leave the lift, the man, also afflicted with a speech impediment addresses her. Fockin' this and fockin' that, he hisses through blackened stumps of teeth; his manner is hostile; he seems to hold her responsible for something or other. Loony, for sure, or perhaps he takes her for an asylum seeker. She is relieved when the happy family shuffle off at the tenth floor. God forbid that she should ever reproduce herself.

Miriam notes the surveillance camera in the top corner of what otherwise is a continuous gleaming surface of textured aluminium panels, the only area that's been refurbished. On the eighteenth floor the lift shudders to a halt and she slips out furtively. The landings on either side are run-down spaces: cracked grey tiles mark out the edges of the floor, the rest having been worn down by years of foot-treads into concrete depressions where leaked water stagnates. At the end of each landing from where a balcony can be accessed is a door to the top flat. What will she do if someone were to open the door – Yes, what do you want? The camera would after all have spied her and who knows, a message may already be circulating through the building, her image reproduced in each flat. She is not sure how these cameras work, or who they are accountable to.

Moira Finnegan: that is the name that springs to mind, the opinionated girl in her tutorial group. That is what she'll say, that she's looking for Moira Finnegan, a friend who has recently moved to the top floor of these flats, although she can't remember which block it is. Moira was the one that sucked up to the mealy-mouthed tutor, a research student who taught the class whilst the professors did who knows what behind closed doors. Clear as daylight she sees from these heights a fresh life without tutorials unfold before her.

Miriam steps out on to the balcony on the West side. What an amazing view, and yes, she would certainly be happy living here. Through the tops of huge old oak trees a silver sliver of river gleams through the disused shipyards, and beyond lie the distant hills or mountains that would have inspired the names of these flats. For all the dilapidation of the building – she kicks against the rusted railings – the grounds below are bright and spacious, with all the magic that an aerial view bestows. Even the abominable cars are grand, parked in paved arcs that look like giant commas punctuating the green. From up here one can see back in time to the architect's drawing board, his vision revealed, realised in the paths and buildings set in a park. Under a bower of trees beside the next building – Miriam cannot read the name of the mountain although it would seem as if all the letters are in place – a family in bright colours is picnicking under grey skies, for the sun has once again disappeared. There are surveillance cameras all along the pathways, but it is good that people go about their business regardless, undeterred by these fascistic measures.

In this park she would be able to think clearly, sitting on the bench under a copper beech, away from the sterility of Holyrood Street with its shaved privet hedges and lack of garden. How odd that the tenements should be considered more desirable than these flats. Here Miriam would meet different kinds of folk, people with whom to discuss the paintings at the base of the buildings. No need for them to find definitive opening lines; there are the living images, expression of raw feeling and desire. There is the very building on whose walls the paintings are executed represented within the paintings, although always with a buttery, beaming sun, and the clichés of doves circling the tower, no doubt in response to the toothless snarls of the natives. How interesting it would be to have a real community, people with whom to talk about the ins and outs of such pictures. Perhaps, she, Miriam, should think of taking up painting herself; after all she had achieved a B for her Higher in Art in spite of her contempt for the moustachioed teacher whose name she refuses to remember.

A door creaks and children tumble noisily out of the top floor flat, accompanied by a woman's tired voice. No, no dinnae youse start playing up. Give it him back Mary. Now. I said, Now.

Miriam imagines that they are too preoccupied to give her the once over. She stands stock still with her back to them. Better to pretend that she belongs there, but when she hears the lift shaft creak, she too goes down. Below in the foyer are a group of men speaking in a language she doesn't know; they do not look like artists.

Cath is in the sitting room listening to a five o'clock news bulletin. If Miriam is not mistaken, her face is damp with hastily wiped tears. What's up, she says briskly; her mother's sentimentality must not be encouraged. Then it comes to her in a flash: the menopause, yes, that would explain the past couple of days. You should see a doctor, she adds, sinking into a chair. Cath will know how you go about getting yourself on the Council's housing list, that is, if she can be distracted from the dated soap opera that is her life.

Cath presses the remote control listlessly. Enough of this, she sighs, God knows where it will all end. Who would have thought that after Apartheid people would turn to such brutality against fellow Africans? Christ, is this what we fought for?

Uh-huh? Miriam says.

Haven't you heard about the migrants from the north being persecuted, killed by people in Gauteng?

As it happens, yes, Miriam had seen the news and the commentary last night. Well, she explains, the government just hasn't delivered its promises; people are as poor as ever, and they see these Zimbabweans and Nigerians as a further drain on…

Cath interrupts, impatient. Yes, of course there are some sectors where little has changed, but what to do now? Today? How to prevent the poor from sinking into further degradation, inflicting further misery on to their fellow sufferers and of course themselves? I know there's no comparison, but just look at the Burnside estate across the road here…

It is Miriam's turn to interrupt. She can't believe her luck, her mother introducing Burnside herself. I was going to ask you, she says, about the estate, about the chances of getting a flat, sharing one if necessary. How do you get yourself on to the council's list? Do you know what the waiting list looks like?

Cath leaps to her feet. Do you have no sense of decency? No

thought for anyone other than yourself? There's history being made before your very eyes and all you can think of is your own precious personal arrangements.

Miriam should have known that the calm, liberal acquiescence about her leaving home was all talk. Clearly her mother resents her plans to leave. Probably can't face living alone. No one on whom to dump the old stories of her days as a resistance fighter. She gives Cath a pitying glance as she leaves the room.

★

Miriam looks at the clock. It is five a.m. She has just been woken up she thinks by sirens, fire engines most likely, since this city seems to be a haven for pyromaniacs. Then, on her way to the lavatory, the telephone in the hall rings. Cath, a voice shouts hoarsely, I've sent the Hukkars round to you. Then the line goes dead.

Cath is up, struggling into her dressing gown. Is it AnnMarie? she asks, Another bloody dawn raid? No sooner has she turned on the kettle than the doorbell rings.

The people at the door are drenched, and in various states of undress. There are three children, and from Mrs Hukkar's torn jacket, worn over lime green pyjamas, juts a prickly twig of flowering hawthorn.

An – an- anMa sa- said to come to you, Mr Hukkar stutters. His face is drawn.

Yes, of course, Cath says, ushering them in.

Miriam, who has pulled a kagoul over her pyjamas, now pulls the hood over her head. What else can she do but pretend that she knows what's going on: the raids by immigration officers trying to arrest asylum seekers; the daily dawn patrols at Burnside, organised by AnnMarie to thwart them; and the telephonic alarm system that warns the immigrants to seek refuge with assigned neighbours. But this time, Mrs Hukkar explains, the police are intent on raiding all the flats, Scots and all, and AnnMarie thought it best to send families out of the building, down the fire stairs. She said she'd come over to Cath's afterwards.

Cath laughs. Oh, AnnMarie will want to see the whole raid

37

through to the end; she loves getting the crowd to stand outside and jeer at the immigration people as they leave the building empty-handed. That's all part of the reward, so last time I showed them how to toyi-toyi African style. How we flummoxed those guys, hey? With arms akimbo and her bum stuck out, Cath starts stomping about the room, ululating a resistance cry.

K-k-k quite so, Mr Hukkar says politely, taking coffee from the tray that Miriam hands round. It is clear that he could not be persuaded to join in, but two of the children are stomping along. The younger, having grabbed the beaded gourd from the sideboard, trumpets into it, Nee-naw, Nee-naw, after the police cars, and quite drowns Cath's Xhosa song.

TEHRAN CALLING

NAM LE

The second announcement woke her. Sarah turned to the window: nothing – night – then, swimming up through the blackness, an image of her face. The cabin lights coming on. She couldn't remember falling asleep. All around her were dark-eyed women dabbing off their makeup, donning head scarves and manteaus in silence, as though beguiled by some lingering residue of Sarah's sleep. Sarah put on her own scarf, felt the knot of cloth against her throat.

The city came up at them like a dream of light. White streams and red, neon lava, flowing side by side along arterial roads; electric dots and clusters of yellow, pink, and orange. She thought of Parvin down there, working her way between those points. With a mechanical groan from the undercarriage the wheels opened out. The plane banked, decelerated, then seconds later they were touching down, roaring to a stop in the middle of a vast, enchanted field. Runways glowed blue in the ground mist. Taxiways green. Lights around them blinking and blearing in the jet fuel haze. Sarah checked her watch: 4 AM local time.

Inside the airport, Parvin was nowhere to be seen. Sarah hurried through the terminal, pursued, it felt, by photographs lining the walls: faces of men in gray beards, black turbans, their expressions strained between benevolence and censure. Despite the hour, the airport was implausibly, surreally busy. Low-wattage light pressed on her nerves as she walked, coercing her body into its familiar anxiety: rushing to work through underground tunnels, the digital alarm still ringing in her ears, toothpaste still bitter on her tongue – suspending herself in the slipstream of other bodies. Staving off sleep. She wore a long black overgarment and black cotton scarf. All the women wore long overgarments and head scarves. This shook her a little – she'd expected more visual disparity. She'd expected to be surprised by it. Around a corner an electronic sign pulsed: IN FUTURE ISLAM WILL DESTROY SATANIC SOVEREIGNTY OF THE WEST. It was too early, and she too tired, to burrow beneath the threat. Keep moving, she told herself.

Large glass windows separated customs from the arrival bay. Retrieving her bags, Sarah noticed a young man watching her through the glass. She stopped, waited for some bodies to interpose, then shuffled out behind them. He was still there. Slight-figured and clean-shaven, nondescriptly dressed. He hadn't taken his eyes off her. A slow warmth rose up from her abdomen. She'd read too many accounts, before coming, about the plainclothes police in this country. She lowered her eyes, withdrawing into her scarf, and then, without warning, he was beside her.

"Sarah." he said.

She froze.

He said, "I am Parvin's friend."

Her posture, she was aware, was one of almost parodic decorum – a sister of the faith, scrupulously observing the veil – but there was no part of her spared to find it funny. She'd barely landed. Now she was shocked awake, her mind instantaneously compacted in fear, fixed on the image of a small dark room ... a metal chair in the middle of it.

"Parvin. You know?"

She didn't speak. What if it were a trick? – to elicit information? An admission of association?

"Come with me," he said. For the first time his English seemed weighted by a heavier accent.

She looked up but he hadn't moved. He reached into his shirt pocket. "Here," he said, and took a step back.

It was a Polaroid. Parvin, her jaw dangling open in the middle of some mischief, one hand brushing back her purple-streaked

hair, the other squeezing Sarah's shoulder. Both their fa⟨
wardly flushed by the candlelit cake before them. Sarah recog.
it from her thirtieth birthday. Five years ago. Parvin had taken
to a sushi restaurant near the Chinatown lions and, after t⟨
complimentary snapshot, had persuaded the waitstaff to sing
"Happy Birthday" in Japanese. They'd filed away, smiling tightly,
harassedly. How hopeless that whole occasion had made her feel,
Sarah remembered – turning thirty – yet even so, looking back
now, she was stifled with nostalgia.

"Good," said the young man. He leaned in closer. "Now.
Please. Come with me."

★

His name was Mahmoud and he was a family friend of Parvin's.
She shouldn't be afraid. Also, he was the leader of the Party.
Parvin worked with him now. Why hadn't she picked Sarah up?
She had been busy with last-minute responsibilities. He spoke
rapidly, in a tone suggesting he didn't want to explain any more
than he already had. He assumed Parvin had told her about the
rally in two days' time.

Sarah sat with him in the backseat, wondering what responsibilities could possibly have kept her friend at this hour. It was
hard to tell whether dawn had broken. A faint glow massed
behind the smog but it could have been the electric ambience of
night – caught and refracted in low-lying haze. In the driver's seat
a heavily stubbled youth named Reza steered their car, an ancient
Ford, like a bullet into the city.

"You have come at a busy time," said Mahmoud.

"Where are we going?" She wound down her window. A warp
of gasoline and exhaust filled the car and she quickly closed it
again. Behind the brief scream of wind she thought she'd heard
the sound of drums. "Where are we meeting Parvin?"

The two men conferred in Farsi.

"You have come during Ashura," said Mahmoud. "Our holiest
week."

She nodded impatiently. Reza glanced up into the rearview
mirror.

"Your hotel is near one of the largest processions," Mahmoud went on. "If you would like to see – if you are not too tired – "

"Hotel? I thought that was just for the visa." Parvin had arranged the letter of invitation from the hotel, had assured her it was just a formality. "I'm staying with Parvin," she said.

The car swerved left. Sarah slid over and smacked into Mahmoud, who flinched, then, as she disengaged herself, smiled stiffly down at his knees. Inexplicably, his reaction riled her. Reza twisted half around from the front seat, made a comment in his skipping Farsi. A short silence ensued, then Mahmoud translated, "He says there are one thousand accidents a day in this city." Reza caught her eye in the rearview mirror and gave her a civic nod. After another silence, Mahmoud said, "We thought it would be better. At the hotel."

"Why?" She frowned, shook her head. "I don't understand."

The lines on his face were so shallow, like lines on tracing paper, and this, with the way his lower lip turned outward, gave him the slightly churlish air of a child. He said, "At least until the rally is over." There was irritation in his voice. "Parvin will explain – she comes to meet us in the afternoon." Then his face closed off completely to her.

Sarah slumped back in the deep seat. As they drove, the sky around them lightened, lifting the concrete landscape – block after block of squat, square buildings – into blue relief. Sarah swallowed repeatedly, trying to clear her throat of its sooty taste. She had no choice – she'd wait for Parvin. Her body felt suddenly spent beneath her clothes. Her head still fumy from the flight, the sleeping pills she'd taken. And now she'd offended this smooth-cheeked boy – this reluctant guide of hers – Mahmoud. She pressed her face against the glass. The city was stilled, caught in the subdued minutes before sunrise. A woman tripped out of a cinder-block doorway, holding her scarf down against the wind. In the distance, the constant shudder of drums. All at once Sarah was overpowered by the strangeness of where she was. Loneliness dropped on her with the speed of a black column.

★

Three months ago, she'd been a senior associate at Pearson, Peelle and Sloss – one of the top-tier law firms in Portland. She'd had a private office with a river view, a private understanding with management with regard to her next promotion, a reservoir of professional goodwill accrued, it sometimes seemed, by virtue of having not yet majorly screwed up. She'd paid off half of a two-bedroom apartment in the Pearl District, exercised almost daily to keep her body in good shape. And – back then – pathetically, she knew – she'd had Paul. She would return from her morning exercise to find him still ensnared in their bedsheets, or shaving behind a blade of light from the bathroom, frazzle-haired and stumbly, seeing her and hauling her body – buzzing and taut and alive – toward his own. He was the aberration of her life: the relief from her lifelong suspicion that she was, at heart, a hollow person, who clung to hollow things.

She unknotted her head scarf. She'd pleaded jet lag as soon as they arrived at the hotel and Mahmoud, who seemed already uncomfortable accompanying her into the lobby, had quickly taken his leave. Upstairs, someone had forgotten to draw the curtains and the room was blanched with golden light. The eastern windows were level with the top of a large plane tree – so close Sarah could reach out and touch its leaves. It cast a fretwork of shadows on the floor.

She removed her long black overgarment and threw it on a chair. Her shirt underneath was drenched. She peeled it off, then her jeans, and abruptly caught a glimpse of her reflection in a bathroom mirror: slender and olive-skinned, a body in accidentally matching bra and underwear. A small wad of undeclared U.S. dollars was gauze-covered and bandaged to the back of her knee. She looked mysterious, glowing – there was a different sun here, somehow; more impersonal. Incandescent. Well, this was what she wanted, wasn't it? She was in the desert now.

They'd met at work. At first he'd been just another good-looking suit in Banking, three floors up, with good teeth, arms that filled out his sleeves when he leaned, the way men always leaned, double-elbowed, on bar counters. He had the salt-and-pepper hair that, on some men, draws more attention to their youth than their age. He was divorced – no kids. He was her professional senior. She'd dealt with him on some statutory debt recovery claims. One day, at Friday drinks, he brought up the last file they'd worked on. Their client had been demanding payment from a company in Chapter 11 but had been low on the list of creditors. The firm had all but counselled forfeit when Sarah developed a submission for priority and, against all expectations, won a good settlement. It had been a tough case. Paul admired her work and said so. Despite her proficiency, work had for so long devolved into sets of empty, unaltering rituals for Sarah that she was capable of registering his comment only as some kind of code. Already, she found herself deferring to him for meaning.

He took her to a seafood bistro near Seven Corners where even the water smelled like mussels. They ordered crabs. Paul rolled up his sleeves and broke open a pincer, his fingers with their perfect square nails glistening in the meat's steam. She found herself transfixed as he slurped the wet flesh. As though to hold up her end of the deal, she tried to eat sexily – imitating the way women on TV pursed their lips, leaving the tip of each morsel visible – but ended up dripping grease down her chin and forearms and onto her blouse. He didn't notice, or seem to. They went on to a small jazz club in an Irvington brownstone that looked, from the outside, like a B&B. The music, breathless and wheezy, mixed with the alcohol, and, when he righted his chair away from her and leaned toward the band, wrists on his knees, his expression almost narcotic in its concentration, she shocked herself by arching over and kissing him on the side of his neck. He turned to her with a look of surprise.

The door of his apartment was cold and hard against her back. She popped up on her toes. His hands were all over her body now. It was dark. He reached under her shirt and pulled it up, over her face. She tilted her head back. The collar caught under her chin. He kissed her through the fabric, roughly, the taste of his mouth salty with the taste of her body. She felt heavy in her legs. The metal of his belt buckle shocking her skin.

"I can't stay," she said.

"I'll stop," he murmured, somewhere around her navel. His fists were tight on her waistband, tugging.

"No." She reached down and outlined his shoulders, tense

with exertion. His tendoned neck. "I mean, I've got a brief due tomorrow." For a moment everything was suspended but the words, the image of her keyboard blue-lit by her screensaver. Why had she said that? He continued below in the darkness. Maybe she hadn't said it aloud. She lifted her legs one by one. "Turn around," he ordered.

She turned around. The air was cold against her bare skin but still she felt woozy with warmth. The music from the jazz club banged around in her head. She had never done this. She had never turned around like that. She was a girl who'd always undressed under the covers and now she was naked in the hallway of an unknown apartment with a man she barely knew behind her.

"Wider."

From an adjoining apartment a telephone started ringing. She heard him undo his buckle, unzip. She could feel the heat of him, her body nervous with want. He spat into his hands and slickened her. A shudder ran through her, was forced from her mouth as noise.

"Wider."

Someone answered the phone, a muffled, stale inflection in counterpoint to his spongy breathing. His wet hands gripping her hip bones. His fingernails. All of a sudden she needed to see him. She needed to see his face. She twisted around and looked at his face. It was creased in anger – his eyes closed – a snarl on his lips. She bit back a cry. She didn't know him. This man who was fucking her. Then she looked again, closely, and realized the look on his face wasn't anger at all.

He was gone when she awoke. The room grown strange in its size, the white glow through the shutters. Except where her body had lain the bed was cold. *Stupid*, she thought, *Stupid, stupid, stupid*. The secretaries would have a field day. Why was she thinking about the secretaries? *Stupid!* She got up, squinting in the dim burn from the windows. Then she saw them –her clothes – neatly folded in a chair. The bastard. Later, she would tell him it was preposterous to think a woman wouldn't interpret the scene as she had. She dressed quickly, quietly, as though under orders. By the time she'd finished she was so shaken that when, on her way out, she saw him at the kitchen counter, still in his boxers, pen in hand, correcting her brief in the light from an open fridge; when he called her name and she heard how it sounded on his lips, it was unfair – an unconscionable situation – because she'd been rendered wholly susceptible and was no longer in any state to resist.

The air-conditioning unit clicked twice, made a rattling sound, whined off. Sarah tried it again then gave up. She lay down on the bed. The sheets were cool, the pillowcases so starched they creased like cardboard. The shadows thrown by the tree boughs against her skin looked like the written language here: half-open mouths, fishhooks, sickle blades, pregnant letters with dots in their bellies. An alphabet refracted in water. She closed her eyes. Again, the faint thud of drums. After a while – unable to sleep – she got up and turned the bath spigot, conscious of the waste but past caring, letting the water run as white noise.

★

The phone rang. Sarah woke up – how long had she been asleep? – into an awful smell: like fruit gone bad, sink water left too long. She struggled to place herself inside it. No one answered when she picked up the receiver, the only sound a faint hum of song. The sun was high outside. She realized now: the smell had worried her since she'd first arrived in Tehran – suppurating as though from some open wound beneath the city.

Three short knocks at the door. She floundered up.

"It's you!" exclaimed Parvin in a hoarse voice, lunging her arms around Sarah's neck. "You made it!" Sarah held on to her, startled by the force of her own relief. They both pulled back. It was disconcerting to see Parvin's face cropped by the black scarf.

"Oh, Sarah." Parvin, smiling steadfastly, seemed on the verge of saying any number of things, but said nothing.

"What's going on?" asked Sarah. "Why can't I stay with you?"

Parvin glanced behind her. In the hallway was Mahmoud, wearing dark slacks with a white shirt buttoned up to his Adam's apple. He looked fleetingly at Sarah, then shuffled his body completely around.

"He told you that?" Parvin lowered her voice: "It was just a precaution."

"A precaution against what?"

Parvin hesitated. "There have been a few arrests." She side-stepped Sarah into the room. "But they tend to crack down during religious holidays. My God, it stinks in here." She swung around. "No – I'll tell you all about it, but right now" – she waved with both hands – "go get your things. We're late."

Sarah dashed into the bathroom. She would save her questions. In the bathtub, the water was cloudy, tinged with mineral colours. She turned off the faucet and suddenly the sound of the outside world flooded in: drumbeats, unmistakable, in every distance, cymbals, the occasional flare of an amplified voice. She thought she heard children's footsteps.

"Sarah!"

The din on the street was astonishing. Noise collected and chafed, it seemed, in the folds of fabric next to her ears. The sky was white, overcast, and beneath it wind gusted, fitfully, as if trapped. They were going to her parents' house for a meeting, Parvin shouted, but first she wanted Sarah to see this. They turned into a chaotic market: shop after shop spilling wares onto the road – hats, shirts and shoes, electronic gadgets that blared a cacophony of tones and trills as they walked past. Sidewalk barrows were packed with green plums and big yellow limes and red-black mulberries, with dates, raisins and nuts of every description. The dull sheen of the sunlight heightened and contrasted the rows of colours.

Parvin turned toward her. "I'm so glad you came." she called out.

Sarah grinned. For the first time since landing she felt completely safe. She was still taking note of the new heft of Parvin's body underneath her robe, the untidy fringe of brown hair – her natural colour! – underneath the hair-clipped scarf. Even her eyes seemed more naturally brown. She looked like a rougher, truer version of herself.

"Where were you this morning?" Sarah asked.

Parvin held up her hand. They rounded another corner and abruptly the air turned thick with deep-throated cries, the crash of cymbals. A mourning procession. It looked, Sarah was stunned to see, exactly how it looked on newsreels: young men straight-backed behind enormous drums; behind them, moving in block step, men clapping their chests, throwing iron chains over their shoulders like dinner jackets. They were all bearded; all – she thought with reflexive guilt – indistinguishable from each other. Men in loose black robes and green headbands. Men with tunics open to their navels. Men naked above the waist – their backs swollen, flayed, slug-shiny in the light.

Sarah let go of her breath. This was why she'd come – to see exactly this – the city as it was – the proof of this place unthinkably outside herself.

Now an enormous square canvas floated down the street, hoisted on two poles and luffing like a sail in the wind. It depicted a black-bearded man. His eyes soulful, mascara-dark, watching everything. The street was full of these pictures.

"Imam Hussein!" shouted Parvin. The loudness of her voice almost tipped it into cheeriness.

He was shown in deep green robes and a black turban, and – with his gentle, cowlike eyes – looked bizarrely like an oriental Jesus. What had Parvin said about bin Laden? That it had to have been a mistake: that no one so soft-spoken, with such kind eyes, with that flossy beard, could have been responsible. It was difficult, sometimes, to tell when she was joking.

"Grandson of the Prophet." That was Mahmoud speaking – he'd caught up with them from behind.

But Parvin was already pushing farther into the mayhem. They came across a low gnarl of bodies: a man with white pants lay on the ground bleeding from his scalp, his hands interlocked around his head as though to improvise a basin. People converged, crouched over him, then kept onward. Sarah realized with horror that they were dipping their sleeves into his blood.

"Why are they –"

The drums drowned her out. She rooted herself within the milling mass and said it again, louder: "Why are they doing that?"

It was a street show extravaganza and she was being scripted, deeper and deeper, into panic. A test, she reminded herself. She could write her own part. Both Parvin and Mahmoud were a short distance ahead, on the opposite sidewalk – Parvin beckoning to her. Parvin, who'd assured her a few months ago it was worth coming just to see Ashura. There was a huge black cauldron behind them. A tarpaulin making the sound of surf as it flapped in the wind – something white and woolly weighing down its centre. Sarah came closer, then shrank back. The carcass of a headless sheep – blood still dribbling, gel-like, from its stump, darkening its matted collar. On the sidewalk, spectators threw up their hands and wailed.

Parvin shoved a plastic cup into her hands. "Tea," she said loudly.

Sarah twisted back toward the parade.

"He is okay," said Mahmoud. He pointed at his head.

"He's not okay, he's bleeding!"

A troop of women and girls poured down the street, coalescing around the prone figure. They were dressed in full black chadors – covering everything but their shoes and faces – and their faces shone out from within their black hoods like beacons of pale grief.

"You are thinking, "What a barbarism," shouted Mahmoud. "You are thinking, "There is much violence in Islam.'"

Some of the women, Sarah noticed, wore white sneakers. They were keening to music that crackled from a ghetto blaster. White and yellow tulips sprang from their hands.

Mahmoud pointed at his head again, a certain shyness in the gesture. Sarah realized her head scarf had slipped down to her neck. She quickly pulled it up over her hair, turned back to face him.

"I was thinking 'Poor sheep… Poor man'."

"The man," he replied with a small smile, "he cuts his head to remember the imam's suffering."

"And the sheep?"

From nowhere, a bearded figure in a black gown and white cap thrust a metal rod in front of her face. She cringed, closed her eyes, then felt the spray of water on her cheek.

Both men enjoyed this. "Perfume," explained Mahmoud, "for pilgrims."

49

Parvin cupped Sarah's elbow in her palm.

The man walked away. There was a metallic tank affixed to his back like a rocket pack. Sarah's face smelled of musk and amber. Dime store deodorant. She made a decision. She swiped the wetness of her cheek onto her fingers and made to flick it at Mahmoud's face, his smooth-skinned jaw.

"Please," he said, taking a step back.

She flushed. "We're all pilgrims," she said.

★

Long before she'd set foot on its streets, this world had already conspired to throw her off balance. When Parvin first told her she'd founded, with typical slapdash resolve, a weekly call-in radio programme agitating for women's rights reform in Iran, Sarah hadn't known what to think. Back then – four years ago – no one did much thinking about Iran. At most, people in her circle were predisposed to a vague solidarity with the country – arising from the sense that any place reprehended by an administration itself so reprehensible couldn't be all that bad.

Parvin had her own ideas. She taught herself how to produce an audio programme at a local college; how to stream it online to a company in Holland, which then broadcast it live, via shortwave radio, into Iran. Shortwave – what did that even mean? Her show, *Tehran Calling*, was live, direct, unrehearsed: its proclaimed mission the complete political, economic and religious liberation of the Iranian woman. Its callers broke the law – risked their lives – every time they called. Sarah indulged her friend's effusions. She'd become used to them. Ever since they'd met in college, Parvin had enthralled herself with one cause or another. What was surprising to Sarah was that Parvin had actually chosen this cause: she'd always been close-lipped – even cagey – about her past in Iran. She'd left as a teenager, Sarah knew that. Her parents had sent her to Europe. Beyond that was a studiedly offhand trail of red herrings: a Swiss boarding school, a German boyfriend, an older divorcé who'd been an offroad racer, a father who'd been a university professor. Sarah could never have predicted that the show would make Parvin a minor celebrity in the Persian reformist movement – let alone that it would pave the way, ultimately, for her re-emigration.

The truth about the show: Sarah had always had trouble taking it seriously. For one, everybody who called in spoke English. Of course it was a show in English, but how could she take seriously the oppression of this far-flung people who were not only English-speaking – but so liberally educated? Who could afford to make these regular international calls? Her misgivings were foolish – she knew that. But on the occasions Sarah had dropped by the studio, she'd repeatedly heard words like *oppression*, lectures laced with jargon and political-science abstractions, and it didn't help that Parvin seemed to absorb, unconsciously, expansively, the heavy Persian accent of her callers. To Sarah it seemed that, as the show grew in popularity, it developed more and more a sense of staged parody.

Once, she'd stepped in near the end of a show and heard a thickly accented male voice ask: "What do you look like?"

Parvin had thrown Sarah a look – a look full of slyness, scorn, self-mockery – and instantly it had dawned on Sarah that Parvin had changed, that she'd drawn away, steadily and for some time, from that side of herself. The side that Sarah knew.

"I think you are ugly," the man said. "Your voice is ugly."

The rest of the hour slid into bewildering invective: Parvin was a monarchist, she was un-Islamic, she was funded by the CIA, she was completely ignorant. Not once did she hang up. She let her callers talk. It wasn't until much later that Sarah learned she'd stumbled on the anniversary of the 1999 student uprisings; then, in the small, too-bright studio that evening, Sarah had struggled to puzzle out her own feelings. She'd never seen her friend like that. Where was the headstrong, irreverent Parvin? the hot-tempered disputant? the career radical who nevertheless prided herself on maintaining professional irony at all times? Where was the strength and variousness on which Sarah had always drawn – and often over-relied? She should say something. What should she say? How to navigate that space between sympathy, tact, unconcern?

A sign above the mixing desk read: PLEASE LEAVE THE STUDIO IN THE SAME CONDITION.

"The thing is," Parvin answered her later, during the drive home, "they're right." It was nighttime now; as she talked, cigarette smoke vented from her mouth and shredded out the open crack of her window. "I was born there but still. You need to be there."

"They shouldn't talk to you like that," said Sarah. She thought of the man's voice – all those voices – faceless and hateful. Those accounts of killings, rapes, finger amputations, related in attitudes that seemed possessive, even petty. If those things were happening, she felt instinctively, they couldn't be happening to those people calling in. Mostly, she realized, what she felt was anger. What she'd meant to say to Parvin was, *You shouldn't let them talk to you like that.*

"It's their right," said Parvin.

"Doesn't it piss you off, though?"

But her friend was resilient, she was preposterous, amazing. Probably there was something wrong with her. Something missing that, in everyone else, assorted actions by the need to be liked and the anxiety that you weren't.

Set in these habits, they grew apart. By then Sarah had met Paul, and Parvin, to Sarah's mind, had reacted gracelessly. She couldn't concede how frustrating it might be for Sarah – watching Parvin sink into a world so at odds with the Iran everyone now heard about: the place populated overwhelmingly by brand-conscious, recreationally drugged youths; riddled with online networking sites and underground dance parties. If there was indeed a tyrannical regime, it seemed the citizenry had opted out of it. This version of Iran, especially being counter-mainstream, struck Sarah as authentic. Parvin, she felt, was being exploited by a native audience that kept insisting – for whatever reason – on its own victimhood.

For a long time Sarah deferred to Parvin's background, probing her friend only lightly about these discrepancies. Later, in efforts to prove the baselessness of Parvin's concerns – the audacious sham of the regime – Sarah began marshalling facts: that during the embassy takeover, for example, people had been bused in from the provinces and hired to burn American flags and shout anti-American slogans in exchange for free food, that they wouldn't start until the cameras were rolling, and if there weren't any video cameras – if only still photographers were present – they wouldn't even bother shouting but just punch the air in silence. It was a country busy with its own deceptions. It neither wanted nor needed Parvin's help.

But Parvin kept on. Three years in, she downgraded, then quit her job with an events coordinating company to dedicate herself to the show. She hired an assistant – with what funds, Sarah never learned. Then she asked Sarah to stop coming to the studio altogether. Sarah's presence and comments, she felt, belittled her efforts. Not long after that they stopped speaking.

"It's what she wants," Paul consoled her.

"What?"

"For us to talk about her. While she suffers, nobly."

Sarah shifted under the bedsheets and thought about her friend, bracketed by her headphones in that dark, windowless studio. It depressed her. "You don't know her at all."

"You know what your problem is?" He traced a path of intersecting loops, a figure eight, around her nipples.

"Which one?"

"You take everything so personally." His face sank into thought. "Can't you see? It's *her* who doesn't know *you* at all."

But what was it Parvin didn't know? Hadn't she seemed sure of her knowledge when she'd declared, during their last conversation, that Sarah had ransomed herself to Paul? That she'd become blind to the needs of those around her – that she now lived a useless life? At the time Sarah had considered those words unforgivable. Then she wasn't sure. For as long as she could remember, she had indeed felt that she hadn't lived in the strong, full-bodied current of her own life; that at some point she'd been shunted to one side, trapped in its shallowest eddies. She was capable of velocity but not depth – there wasn't enough to her. It was Paul, when she met him – as gradually she got to know him – who seemed to suggest the possibility of a deeper, truer life. He could anchor her. That was what Parvin could never understand. That it could actually be – had actually been – Sarah's choice.

She made the decision to love him and she did. He walked into a room and stood still. His face clouded when he planted himself behind her, bobbed above paper bags as he carried them up the stairs. When he cooked for them, he rolled up his sleeves and tipped and tilted the frying pan in a half-haute style that never failed to delight her. When he made their bed, he made it a point to billow the sheet out over the mattress in a single flourish. She loved the striations of his character – how, at work, he became serious, taciturn, giving himself over to the duties of the profession in the old sense. They lived together, worked together. Once a year they visited his family home in New Hampshire. It was there, in that large house in that large clearing, that Sarah finally realized how much Paul's character had been governed by his parents' easy formality; there, watching them attend their shared days, that she'd allowed herself to extrapolate – impossible not to! – her own future with their son.

Her first visit, she'd endlessly explored the wooded backyard that gave onto a lake the locals insisted on calling a "pond". One hot afternoon she convinced Paul to swim with her to the opposite shore. The water was the one place she felt more comfortable, could lead the way. Unexpectedly – charmingly – he was a nervous swimmer, and she set a slow pace. They swam a good mile or so, then pulled themselves onto a boulder. The rock almost too warm. Once the sludge and sand had settled, the water over the edge became so clear that they could see all the way down. Gnats and dragonflies skated the liquid surface. Beneath, shapes of fish trolled the leaf-tramped bed. Sarah ducked her head underwater. When she opened her eyes she caught sight of two brown-spotted trout within arm's length; she tracked their languid movements until suddenly a sleek, almost metallic gleam of black and white crossed her vision; she turned, saw – bewitchingly – the beak, the folded, streamlined wings – it was a loon – gliding steadily into the cool depths. She spluttered to the surface, mute with excitement, and saw Paul lift his head from the rock and smile at her as if he understood completely, and right then she knew, cross her heart, in all her life, that she'd never been so happy.

Parvin left for Iran. The news, when it came a year ago, seemed abstract and out of place in her life. At last, part of Sarah admitted that she had misjudged her friend, had taken her at far less than her word. But the rest of her – the part given over to Paul – took ever more pleasure from him and, in her mind, day by day, proffered it to Parvin as rebuke.

★

"This morning," said Parvin. They were walking to the car, back along the smoke-drab streets. Mahmoud locked in step behind them. "What can I tell you about this morning?"

On both sides of the road, multi-story walls had been painted over in gaudy murals: Shi'ite saints, mope-faced martyrs in army uniforms, garlanded with flowers and butterflies and rainbows. Publicly-rendered paradises. Beneath one mural a thoroughfare was strung with fairy lights, an Internet café crowded with youths. Walking past, Sarah glimpsed girls in heeled boots, girls with colourful hijabs, sunglasses perched on top of them.

Here she was, she thought – with Parvin – in the place itself. She'd bought a ticket – that was all it took! – and stunningly, almost unimaginably, she was *here*.

That morning, Parvin explained, while Mahmoud was picking Sarah up from the airport, Parvin had met with members of a sympathetic group. A drama company from one of the city's smaller universities. It was urgent, they'd said. They needed to speak to someone high up in the Party.

Mahmoud walked behind them, leaving a buffer between his body and theirs.

"I thought the worst, of course. They'd found us out. Or they were gathering all their people to attack us on Thursday." She looked around, askance. "It's happened before."

They passed a jewellery shop glittering gold, silver, crystal. Out front, a group of men were arguing animatedly. They all had the same puffed-up hair, all wore what looked to be hand-me-down suits from the eighties. Across the street, Sarah saw the upper half of men's bodies draped over scooter handlebars, the bottom half of their faces darkened by short beards. Mahmoud caught her eye and held it coolly for a moment.

"What it was," said Parvin, "was they'd put together a play. That was the big secret."

55

"A play?"

"Oh, Sarah – you should have seen it." She pinched up the thigh of her robe as she stepped over a reeking culvert. Ruts ran all over the road and sidewalk, trickling waste into the gutters. "One of them had a little sister. Thirteen years old. She wanted to be an actor too." Parvin scaled her voice back. "Last month they arrested her – for 'acts incompatible with chastity'."

"What's that mean?"

"Then they held her for two weeks of tests and interrogation." She spun around to face Sarah. "Were you searched? At the airport?"

Sarah shook her head. Parvin nodded, walked on. Unbidden, a particular case from her pre-travel research surfaced in Sarah's mind. Zahra Kazemi, Canadian journalist, detained for taking photos during a protest – then beaten, with a guard's shoe, into a coma. She remembered the picture she'd seen: a late-middle-aged woman, her baggy chocolate-coloured sweater lending her a girl-like air. She remembered the camera hanging from her neck, its black lens a well beneath her own calm, deeply settling face.

"Last week," said Parvin, "she was hanged. This little girl. All this is in the play. It's sentimental, and a bit slapstick, I'll admit, for a tragedy – but they only had a week to throw it together." A steeliness Sarah had never heard before now reinforced her friend's voice. Parvin flipped her thumb – a hitchhiker's gesture – behind her, toward Mahmoud. "But he's not a fan."

"Too much!" said Mahmoud. Sarah turned. His Adam's apple jogged pronouncedly above his collar. "I said it is not a play for Ashura."

"It's the perfect play for Ashura," Parvin spat. "It's a very religious play."

They'd reached the car. Parvin stood by the passenger door and stared directly at Sarah. "Those *men*," she said, curling her mouth on the word, "those men of God, do you know how they enforce God's law?" She'd brought her voice under control, but tension clenched her shoulders and neck. "They kidnap this girl on an immorality charge. Then they test her – but find out she's still a virgin."

"Parvin," Mahmoud implored. "Please get in the car."

"So what do they do? They marry her, so they can rape her. They rape her – so they can kill her – so she won't go to heaven, where all the virgins go." Her nostrils flared in the middle of her rough, square face. "Men of God," she said.

A block away, drums were beaten as though into the ground, trembling the very concrete. Mahmoud's eyes searched the street. To her surprise, Sarah felt a swell of sympathy for him – even as she found herself exhilarated by Parvin's rage. No one else she knew, it occurred to her, would ever dare speak so critically of Islam. Parvin got in the car. She looked down at her lap for a long time. Then, in a softer, effortfully lighthearted tone, she said, "And what about Sarah? If she has to wait till after Ashura, she'll miss the play."

"How long are you staying?" demanded Mahmoud. He pinned her with his gaze.

Sarah smiled weakly. "Six days."

The engine clattered to life and they pulled away, the parade diminishing behind them. Mahmoud drove and didn't talk. Parvin was quiet now too. They merged with traffic on a busy one-way street and seemed to drive directly into smog. Sarah looked out, her head as clouded as the air, the thoughts within it churning shallow and fast. It felt inconceivable she'd been here only a few hours. She slackened her attention and almost convinced herself she was home again: slate-gray sky, concrete-walled compounds, poured-cement yards, a roofline rife with billboards and signs. But wherever she looked, just underneath the outside of things, something was always slightly off: ordinary buildings listed towards, or away from, one another – their lines never quite plumb; straight roads turned into alleys wending into dead ends. And words – words everywhere – on trucks, street signs, T-shirts – seemed like language that had been melted, meandering up and down like quavers and clefs on invisible staves. The car climbed to higher ground. Sarah stuck her whole head out the window, letting the wind crunch her scarf against her ears. On every other corner she thought she heard an English-speaking cadence – recognized someone from home – but then the realization set in. Parvin was here. Otherwise she was alone.

People looked at her and understood that. She was completely extraneous.

As they repaired to the quieter, more affluent boulevards of northern Tehran, it felt like they were entering a different country. At one point they crested a rise and ahead, through a green canopy, materialized the full spread of the Elburz Mountains, stately and snowcapped, slopes dappled with sun and cloud and shadow. Mahmoud turned up a narrow street. They stopped in front of an old, weatherworn villa, which, Sarah was astonished to learn, belonged to Parvin's family.

What she noticed first, entering the room, were the women seated at the long dining table. They'd shed their robes, four or five of them, and their hair was uncovered. Several men were present, too, standing across the room next to a set of ornate sofas. Mahmoud immediately joined them. Platters of bread, goat cheese, pistachios and yoghurt were laid out on tables.

Conversation paused when Sarah walked in.

"This is Sarah Middleton," announced Parvin, pushing her scarf back onto her neck like a hood. "Who I told you about. My best friend." She repeated the introduction – more emphatically, it seemed – in Farsi.

A couple of the women nodded to Sarah. "Come, sit down," said one. She sat by herself at the far end of the dining table.

"Thank you."

The woman poured tea into a glass shaped like an egg timer and handed it to Sarah. She slid a vase of pink-blue gladioli out of the way. "My name is Roya," she said. She was young but there was a subtle dourness about her face that weighed on her features. Her body was stout, small-breasted, and she wore a tight T-shirt with a Chinese character embossed on it. It seemed on her almost a parody of youthful fashion. She said, "So you are the one."

"The one?"

"The one whose heart is broken." She peered into Sarah's face. "You must forgive my English."

Sarah turned sharply to Parvin at the other end of the table. She was absorbed in conversation with the group of women. Sarah

58

turned back. Who was this woman? What did she know? Her comment felt to Sarah almost spiteful. Now Roya leaned in closer.

"I have wine too," she said.

Sarah gave a terse shake of the head.

"It is made by my parents. I know where they keep it upstairs. And their opium, too – if you prefer."

Mahmoud said something aloud and immediately the men unbunched and came over to the dining table. He was the shortest of them all, Sarah saw, yet they all treated him with noticeable deference. Sarah stood up. She felt like being alone.

"No," Parvin called out from across the table, "Stay. You should stay."

"I will translate for her," said Roya. Parvin smiled at both of them before turning back to her discussion.

Something occurred to Sarah. "You live here?"

Roya lifted her hand to her mouth. "She did not tell you?" She rested her chin in her palms – an awkwardly coquettish effort to frame her face. "I am her sister."

Sarah sat down and sipped her tea. She felt acutely unsettled. It was in keeping with Parvin to withhold details, but all this? – this sister from an erstwhile life? This baroque villa? What else hadn't her best friend told her?

"Are your parents here?"

"They are away because of the rally." On seeing Sarah's expression, Roya amended, "I mean, they are in Turkey for vacation. They give us the house for the rally."

The meeting began. Mahmoud spoke first and others – in particular, Parvin – interjected. It soon became clear, as Roya confirmed during the course of her choppy, digressive translations, that they were again arguing about the play. Parvin wanted to stage the reenactment – in the square where the rally would be held – of the young girl's torture and execution. Mahmoud said it would be too dangerous. The square would be watched by religious militia. Such a reenactment would mock the official passion plays of the Battle of Karbala. Sarah tried to concentrate but she felt, as Roya jawed in her ear, the room, the crowd of strangers, their heated back-and-forth – everything – all receding from her, as though she were in her mother's house again, watching the plants in front of the living room window curl into chalky remnants of themselves. Parvin was gesticulating. Sarah, watching, now felt a delicate tenderness toward her: she had, at least, acknowledged Sarah's heartbreak – if only to her sister. She'd said to her sister that Sarah was the one. Had she also told Roya that for the last three months – since Sarah had quit her job – she'd crawled back to her mother's house? Eating, not talking, blanking out and coming to with undirected terror? Awakening constantly as if from afternoon naps into darkness? Even now, those months seemed to Sarah a dim fantasy. Those honest, initially unbearable conversations she'd had with Parvin about Paul all seemed suspensions of lived memory. They'd talked like suitors, careful with one another, and in the end, when Parvin had extended the invitation, it hadn't been assurance or exhortation that had convinced Sarah to come to Tehran but the note of vulnerability she'd detected in Parvin's voice when she'd stated, simply, *I want you to see what I've been doing.*

Someone was saying her name. She blinked, focused on Mahmoud. He said in English, "Sarah, what do you think?"

Everyone watched her silently. She hauled her mind back to its present circumstance: the rally, the play. She sensed Parvin glowering in her direction.

She said, "Well, if it's dangerous – "

Mahmoud's mouth twisted up at one corner.

Parvin broke in, "What does she know? She's only been here half a day."

"And how long have you been here?"

"Mahmoud," said one of the women.

"No," he declared. "Was she here in 1999? When we went out on the streets and and – and Hassan and Ramyar and Ava were taken? And she" – pointing to Parvin – "was in her radio station in America, telling us to go out on the streets?"

Parvin said, "I didn't have a show in 1999."

"Last June," muttered a young, dark-haired woman.

"I'm as politically committed as anyone here."

"She was not here in 1999," said Mahmoud, "and she was not here last June."

Parvin turned directly toward him. "I'm here now," she retorted, but her voice inflected upward, as if unsure whether or not it was asking a question.

"And now, for her, we should defame our religion? When she understands nothing of it?"

"Forgive him," said Roya. She looked sideways at Sarah.

"Why did you come?" a man's voice demanded.

For a moment no one spoke, then Sarah realized, all at once, that he was speaking to her. She broke off a piece of bread and dipped it in yoghurt. It would be folly, she knew, to engage someone in such an aggressive frame of mind.

Parvin turned towards Sarah. Her face had an odd, hollowed-out look to it. She said, "She came to visit me."

Mahmoud held up two fingers in a dogmatic manner, his head and neck gone rigid. He started intoning in Farsi.

"The imam comes to Karbala with fewer than one hundred men," translated Roya, her tone official, impersonal, "to sacrifice himself to the army of Yazid."

Mahmoud floated his gaze over to Sarah.

"He is – how do you say it? – beheaded. He dies – for who? For mothers and for daughters. And now we are to spit at his face?"

Parvin, seething, replied in a low voice, in Farsi.

"He does not die for the little girl," said Roya.

Mahmoud spoke again. Roya said, "This week is to mourn the imam."

She waited for Parvin to finish speaking, then said, "Who will mourn the little girl?"

Then, once Mahmoud had spoken, she lifted her hand and flicked her fingers, unconsciously mimicking him, and said, "One has nothing to do with the other."

Roya led her to an upstairs study that smelled strongly of wood lacquer. The window had wooden shutters and, behind those, thick milk-coloured drapes. A small writing desk fronted the view. A single bed against the wall. Roya went in and shuttled the curtains to either side, letting the sunlight strafe in.

"There is a bath," she said. For a moment Sarah was confused.

Then Roya opened a semi-concealed, recessed door and showed Sarah into a bathroom as large as its adjoining room. The toilet, Sarah noticed, was Persian-style – a porcelain-lined hole with a hose adjacent. Through the walls Sarah heard the distinct sound of a BBC broadcast.

"You have satellite?" she asked.

Roya smiled at her almost maternally. Then she crossed her arms over the Chinese character on her chest and rocked back on her heels. Her face became pinched and brisk.

"Parvin says you come for the rally."

"Yes," Sarah said carefully.

She emitted a dry chuckle. "Parvin is excited about these things. Very easily. Always. Like the play."

The scene downstairs came back to mind. "Does that happen a lot?" Sarah asked. "Parvin and Mahmoud, I mean."

"Yes," said Roya. Then, "No, not like that."

An impulse stirred within Sarah. "What do *you* think about the play?" When Roya didn't reply, she quickly pressed on: "You must be very happy to have Parvin back."

But Roya was thinking about something else. Finally she said, "Mahmoud does not talk about it." She stood, arms crossed, absolutely still. "In 1999 his brother was shot. In the square where the rally will be."

Sarah exhaled.

"And then his father, who is an important cleric here – how do you say it? – denied him. As his son. In the mosque."

At that, Roya pushed past Sarah back into the study, then hesitated by the desk. Her stance was guarded now, as though waiting to be dismissed. "Parvin likes it in America, yes?" She pronounced it *Amrika*. Without waiting for an answer, she said, "Parvin wanted to go, always, as a child." She leaned forward. Sarah realized she was being confidential. "I could have gone too, you know."

Late afternoon light streaked in, contoured Roya's face in sharp, ambiguous planes. All at once Sarah comprehended the woman in front of her. She was the one who'd stayed behind. She'd stayed, toiling the same unspoken trench of sacrifice so that her sister could escape.

"The play," said Roya, "it seems like punishment." She lingered on the word. "But who is it punishing?"

"Is it too late?" asked Sarah. "For you to leave?"

Roya stared at her for a moment, then her face dissolved into a slippery mess that had a smile in it. "I think about it," she said. "But why would I leave now?" She giggled into her fingers. "This is the most exciting time. If I leave now, what if I miss something?"

★

When Parvin was fourteen, her family had long been marked as subversives by the revolutionary committees. Although they were religious – and had originally supported the revolution – her parents had been forced into hiding and her two older brothers into the front lines of the war.

Sarah started. She hadn't known about any brothers.

This was the war, Parvin went on, where thousands of boys cleared minefields by walking over them, clutching plastic keys to heaven; where soldiers died in Iraqi chemical attacks because the beards they had grown to demonstrate their faith made it impossible for them to achieve proper seals with their gas masks. Parvin fell silent. She made no more mention of her brothers.

They were sitting in one of the villa's upstairs studies. Outside the window a busted streetlamp flashed, at long intervals, on and off. Sarah only noticed when the brightness was doused – the world steeped a grade darker.

Meanwhile, said Parvin, they were bombarded in Tehran not only by missiles but by announcements, victory marches – all extolling the glories of martyrdom. This was 1988. One day, a bomb razed their neighbours' apartment building. Her best friend lived there, and her cousins' family. She rushed over but already – even before the ambulances arrived – the wreckage had been blocked off by *basiji* in their red headbands. They barked out propaganda from their motorbikes. Parvin ran forward but was immediately knocked to the ground. Her ears were still ringing from the explosion. No one moved to help as one bike after another skidded inches from her head, spraying dirt and dust into her face. *No crying!* they shouted. *Death to Saddam!* they shouted. *Death to America!* It was in that moment, Parvin said, that she'd known she would have to get out of the country. The decision tormented her – her parents had already made it clear they could never leave their homeland. Her own loyalty, however, was used up. Or maybe it was greater than theirs. She didn't care where she went – to America, if those devils reviled it so much. All she knew was that she couldn't allow this place any further claim over her.

By the time Parvin finished her account, night had fallen and the broken streetlamp lit their room in long, freakish strobes. The wind had picked up and the dark world outside now seemed suggestive of peril: window boards banging against frames, cans scraping themselves jerkily, as though injured, across the roads. Looking up, it was unnerving to Sarah how fast the clouds seemed to move across the nimbus of the moon.

Parvin murmured, "I'm sorry about what happened at the meeting."

Sarah shook it off. She glared at Parvin. "Why didn't you tell me?"

"I didn't want to be defined by it. The exotic friend with the traumatic past." Parvin switched on a lamp. "You know how it is. Especially now."

"But your brothers."

Parvin averted her gaze.

"Your sister. I'm your friend. You could've told me."

A strange, abstracted pity sought its level within Sarah. For years she'd yearned to hear this story – this missing piece of Parvin's past – but now that she had, she felt no closer to her. She was confused. Hadn't she come here, in part, to make sense of Parvin's choices? And didn't this – the deaths of her brothers – now offer up that final sense?

"My sister?" Parvin looked blank, then started bemusedly to smile: "Roya? She's not – she was married to my elder brother." She broke off. "I've never really known her."

Outside, the wind squalled harder, skimming water up from unseen surfaces and spraying it through the shutters. Parvin got up and closed the window. Sarah saw her face, as she did so, setting inwardly.

Parvin turned around. "They all talk about needing to be here," she said. "But I was here."

In a way, Sarah envied them their pasts – Parvin, Roya – joined even by atrocity and privation, a shared past of such moment that they'd been forced, in separate ways, to flee from it. Mahmoud, who could reach meaningfully back to mythic battles. What did Sarah have? A childhood dim and distant, a thing half chewed and incomplete as though first used up by someone else. Memories of her parents, their rubbed-out faces. Only Paul remained – his vividness constant, hurtful, taunting. He walked into a room and stood still. Her past had never offered her any real excuses.

"Anyway," said Parvin, "they're all hypocrites. They'd all get out if they had the guts."

Sarah hesitated. She thought of what Roya had said earlier. "Things are really that bad?"

"They've lost their nerve, is what it is. I'm so sick and tired of all this consultation. All this uprising by committee. All we do is hedge and prevaricate. The other side doesn't prevaricate. Ask that thirteen-year-old girl if they prevaricate."

She was speaking now as though to an interviewer – as though into a microphone or megaphone. Pacing the small study. Her two brothers, Sarah reminded herself, had vaporized on the western fields – but already that seemed too easy an explanation. She wanted a deeper sense. Parvin had left here young – returned of age, zealous and single-minded. All those prodigal years in Portland – the biggest part of her life – what had they meant to her? Had they been anything more than personal wilderness? And what, then, of Sarah?

"Look at what they do," Parvin said. "And we let them get away with it. We bend over backward – just to not offend their religious sensitivities. And the women – " she splayed open her fist in disgust – "all talking about equal rights, equal legal status, under sharia law. Under an Islamic state. All bullshit."

An image of Mahmoud came into Sarah's head: his two fingers pointing up vatically, like a mock gun, while he preached. She asked, "Do they know? The drama group?"

"Know what?"

"That you're not putting on their play."

Parvin considered her curiously. "If they want to put it on, who's going to stop them?" A gust of wind leaned against the house, creaking the walls in their joints. Parvin dipped her chin, then vigorously shook her head as though to cut short Sarah's protests. "So maybe they won't do it on the stage. Or as part of the official programme."

"I just don't understand," Sarah burst out, "what it's meant to do."

Parvin stared at Sarah, her mind shifting through its reactions.

Sarah said, "If the play's only going to antagonize people, religious people—"

"Remember the parade today?"

"During their most important religious holiday—"

"All those religious people, mourning together, right? Devout." Parvin squared round to face her. "Except – when you're in it, you realize it's more than that. I'll tell you what it is. It's sexual. That's how these things work here. All day, every day – it's don't do this, don't do that. Then – in God's name – step into one of these things and cop a feel." She strained, strenuously, intricately, for the words. "It's all a con," she said. "Step in – then step out and tighten your veils."

Sarah had been holding her breath. Now, as she let it out, she sensed that a mood in her head had cooled and hardened. "You know," she said, "what you're doing. All this. It doesn't mean anything to me." Her own calmness surprised her.

Parvin stopped, turned away from her. "Listen," she said. She took hold of her voice, "It's a shock at first, I know. But you'll see. Thursday—"

"I want to understand," Sarah continued, "I do. That's why I came here. But it doesn't make sense to me, not emotionally, not even in an intellectual way."

Parvin stood still for a while, then went over to the window and looked out. Wind, on the other side of the glass, absorbed the light, released it. From somewhere in the house rose the scent of burnt tea. Sarah waited, feeling the grief of a bygone situation, the deep-seated loneliness, well up into her like a drug. She'd made her choices years ago. They both had. How could they think to undo them now?

"Is this about Paul?" said Parvin.

Sarah didn't say anything.

Parvin thought for a moment, then said, "We can talk about it. Let's talk about it."

"Why does it have to be about Paul?"

Parvin's face contracted. "Isn't it?"

But there it was, in her voice – the habitual undertone, the unsaid charge that had tolled out between them ever since Parvin started the radio program. That Sarah's relationship with Paul wasn't worth talking about. That it had always been a luxury, ill-used and underappreciated, which Sarah had somehow snatched from the finite resources of other women – these women – and then squandered.

"Don't worry," Sarah said. "I won't make you talk about him."

It started raining. Standing at the window, her back to the room, Parvin continued, "You must be tired. Roya prepared the guest room for you." She stayed standing there. Then she added, "I always thought Paul was fine. It was you who made things unbearable for yourself."

"I'm sorry," said Sarah, "that my problems—" she broke off, her throat constricting – "that they were never as impressive as yours."

"God," said Parvin, a sneer in her voice, "you haven't changed at all." She started walking away. At the door she spun around. "You know," she said, "this isn't all just make-believe for me." Her voice was unnaturally flat. "I just opened myself to you."

Sarah looked at her wretchedly, with the full force of accusation. "I know."

Parvin left. Sarah stayed and listened to the rain. She felt crushed, completely enervated. No matter where she turned, everything she touched, she ruined. Moments later – though it seemed too early to sleep – she crept out and closed the door behind her, cautiously, as though leaving a hospital ward. She went to find her bed.

★

Roya was wrong: it wasn't Paul who had broken her heart. Her

67

heart had come already impaired. From the beginning she'd led a life of what seemed to be mere self-maintenance. She'd calibrated herself to be above average in all the average ways: running down the hours, the feasible commitments, the ready consolations of work and sleep. She'd built her life, elegantly, around convention – conventional aspiration, conventional success – and was continually astounded that no one saw through the artifice – no one recognized Sarah Middleton as all falsework and nothing within. Only Parvin had sensed this, she felt, and back in college had accepted Sarah into her friendship with as few questions as she wanted asked of her. It wasn't that they weren't intimate, or equal – more that Sarah, by nature, found it easiest to fall in with her, and had always been grateful for it.

Of course, Paul complicated everything. Parvin could never understand that for Sarah, being with him was, in a slanted way, like watching TV – one of the few things capable of dragging her, temporarily, to a deeper plane of living. He took her conventionality and gave it depth, lustre, definition. How had that happened? Even now, her memories of him dulled everything else. Their last morning: the broad-branched maples catching and holding the last of the dew, running it down their boughs and bodies in streaming rills. How, underneath the canopy, the air was cold, below the frost point, and the cordgrass as she waded through it crackled and chinked like Christmas paper.

They broke up where, for Sarah, they'd truly begun. On their last trip to New Hampshire, in that held-breath space in a rare argument where they could be absolutely honest with each other, she'd asked – in a low voice as though to forestall any interest in his answer – whether he wanted to leave her.

He'd paused. Mulling it over, as if it were a trick question.

"Please tell me," she said. "You have to tell me. Do you?"

He said, "No." But his face had caved into a deep frown.

The next morning, ankle-deep in the wet grass, she'd thought over their life back in Portland – their shared apartment, their shared work – how it had seemed so tenable for so long. Years of her life. She turned to look at the blank-faced house and imagined him inside, asleep, buffered by his safe, solid childhood, his imperturbable parents – their mess of shared assumptions – and it occurred to her that maybe she had in fact simulated their entire relationship. Maybe she'd lived it on both sides. What did she really know about him? – about how he felt about her? The front door of the house opened and he came out swathed in one of his family bathrobes.

"Sarah?"

He crossed the back lawn in his slippers.

"It's freezing out here," he said. "Come on."

She watched him approach. The grass washed into a bright green that was full of light, that had yellow in it. Behind him, black clouds sprouting on the horizon, flying fast and low toward them, shaving the tops of trees. He stopped at the edge of the lawn. Then she saw it in his face. With a visceral hitch that was at least part relief, she thought of all the things that would happen now – the crushing logistics of moving out, parcelling out property, navigating a shared workplace – all the wearying, recursive conversations she would be fated to have.

Paul took his bathrobe off and wrapped it around her. Underneath, he wore boxers and a T-shirt, and the sight of it tore her apart.

What had been real and what not? What must she hold onto, what release? Sarah sat on her bed, staring out into the dimly glowing night. Low, grey, boxlike buildings stretched away into brown slums and behind those, Mahmoud had told her, was the salt desert. Dasht-e Kavir. From out that expanse came music all night, parched, tattered – drums, always, but also fragments of a man's voice in harrowed mourning. Once Sarah heard the theme from *Titanic*.

In the beginning it had been terrifying. Her working life she'd spent assigning tasks to units of time; how, then, could she spend all her time *not* thinking about him? She quit her job, moved into her mother's house. She'd saved enough that money was never an issue. It had been far easier than she'd expected to leave work – but surviving a vacant day seemed impossible. She couldn't cast her life so far. It was a matter of hours – minutes, really, and through those minutes it had been Parvin who had talked her on, coaxed her to apprehensible distances. They'd pored over her pain together – Sarah, all the while, shirking the suspicion that her friend was now only ever present for her pain. What had been real? When had Sarah truly been happy? Here – now – in this dark villa – her life again revealed its fibre to her. Work: an overcast spread of clocked-in hours. Paul: streaks, dyed strands of memory, unravelling at every touch. To think about it now, the closest she'd ever come to real happiness had been by herself: swimming at the local indoor pool before work. She'd always liked the silence of new morning, the crisp smell of chlorine, the high stained-glass windows that, during summer, filtered the light through like bottled honey. Sometimes, when she was first to arrive, the rectangle of unbroken water shone with the hardness and sheen of copper. She liked the companionship she shared with the other swimmers – all serious swimmers at that hour – the feeling of being alone, unrequired to commit any of the compromises required of human interaction, and yet a part of them; her mere presence the stamp of her belonging. Here she belonged. She liked standing on the blocks, goose-pimpled, second-guessing, and then the irretractable dive into cold water – the sheer switch of it against her skin – she was wet now, cold, her hair wet, and there was nothing to do but to swim herself warm. Lap after lap she would swim: pure sound and feeling; matching the rhythm of her strokes to the pace of her breathing, the ribbed circuit of air through her body. Conditioning herself into a kind of peace. Then, afterwards – home.

★

Sarah woke first the next morning. She ran the bath, turned the bathroom light on, then off again. The water reflecting the bone-dull sky. She slipped out of her underwear and into the cold water.

Beneath her, the house roused slowly into sound. She lay in the tub, studying the high, molded ceilings, taking in the scents of lacquer and rosewater. She'd made it through the night. Was Parvin awake? Sarah felt towards her now a mild, civilized remorse – as if all her antipathy had exhausted itself the previous night.

As she dressed, the sound of amplified stereo static, followed by a haunting ululation, piped through the street bullhorns. The call to prayer. She went to the wood-shuttered window, looked out through the web of large leaves. The sound touched a deep chord within her. For the first time, she strove to imagine the cleanness of belief that could pull all those foreheads to stone, unwaveringly, five times a day. What was the lie? That you could change your life? She looked out, watching the unknown city roll out before the new sun, its dazzling labyrinth of streets and walls, its villas and bazaars, the evil vizier cast down for good into the valley and the smog burned off to unveil magnificent Damavand – vast and near, seamed with snow and meltwater. It was a two-minute peace – she knew that – but she allowed it.

"I know, it still gets me too."

Sarah turned around and saw Parvin in the doorway. She wore, uncharacteristically, a long, fluid, green dress, and her mouth was pressed tight.

Sarah started to speak but Parvin held up her hand. She sat down on Sarah's bed. The call to prayer continued, the man's voice so elongated, so reedy, it sounded like an instrument.

"There's a word in Farsi," Parvin said, "*Khafeghan*. It means a feeling where you can't breathe. A kind of claustrophobia." Parvin lifted her face and stared straight ahead. "You hear it used a lot over here."

Sarah tried to repeat the word. "I think I understand," she added.

Parvin shifted on the mattress to face Sarah. "Listen," she said, "This is my work. This is what I do now." She made an effort to smile, and then she did. "It's enough that you're here."

"I can't believe it. That I'm here. You're here."

Parvin thought for a moment, then said, "I won't lie to you. Mahmoud thinks you shouldn't come tomorrow."

"What do you think?"

"There's something else," said Parvin. "One of our members isn't answering his cell phone." She jutted out her jaw, then closed her mouth again. "It's probably nothing, but you never know."

Sarah looked at Parvin, newly surprised by the green dress –

gladdened, somehow, by how obliviously she wore it. A vestige of peace abided in Sarah. She wanted to share it with her friend but before she could figure out what to say, Parvin had already stood up and left the room.

★

All day the Party convened downstairs. Sarah was glad to keep to herself, perusing books in the study – mainly German books on art and architecture. She found the satellite television and sated herself on current events, most of which seemed irrelevant and repetitive. She watched clouds move across the mountains. Jet-lagged, she fell asleep.

Late in the afternoon, Roya barged into her room. Sarah barely recognized her at first, fully arrayed as she was in robe and head scarf.

"Parvin is gone," she said. She looked at the cell phone in her hand. "Reza says she is going to the square."

"Is she okay?"

Roya shrugged, her expression indistinct. "He says she is meeting with the drama group. He went with her to help."

"Wait," said Sarah. "Where are you going?"

"I am going out." She puckered her lips, shot Sarah an astute look. "I think Mahmoud is driving to the square."

It was almost dark when they left. The motorway was clogged – cars like theirs – wide and metal and box-nosed. They turned down a one-way street straited on both sides by canals. Buses belched out charry exhaust. Sarah looked and spotted men with kerchiefs over their faces, women with rearranged scarves. A city of bandits. Suddenly a bus – going the wrong way – roared straight at them. She gasped, closed her eyes, then realized they were okay. The contra-flow lane, said Mahmoud, muttering his reassurances.

Neither of them wanted to talk about Parvin. They talked instead about the program for the rally. Sarah asked him about his father. He hesitated, then told her his father was a high-ranking cleric, one rank below ayatollah – here you decided for yourself when you were ayatollah – but his, Mahmoud's, own religion was more complex.

He was born after the revolution. What did that mean? It meant he was supposed to feel a certain way.

He and his father no longer talked.

"I forgot you were a lawyer," he said wryly.

The Party stood for civil rights. That was all. It was not anti-Islam. Nor was it anti-America. After 9/11 they'd come out with the other thousands and did she know what they said? They said, *Death to terrorism!* They said, *Death to bin Laden!* They said, *America, condolences, condolences.*

Abruptly he turned to her. "Was Parvin like this when you knew her?"

"Like what?"

"Like she cares for nothing. For no one."

"What are you talking about?"

They rumbled across a low bridge. The water below soupy and junk-filled.

"She's trying to help," said Sarah. Without fully understanding why, she felt – in that moment – that before Mahmoud she would defend Parvin to the very end. She owed her that much.

"And you?"

She laughed uncertainly. "Don't ask me about politics," she said. "I'm just here for her. Moral support."

"Moral support," he repeated.

They parked the car and started walking. A drizzle came down and made the concrete dark around them. At last they reached the edge of a large square. It shone with the changing light of a thousand candles. In the radiance Sarah could see that stalls had been set up in parallel rows and a stage erected at the far end. There was movement on the stage. Two large portraits of the black-bearded martyr bannered down on either side. Above the ground glow, trees had been hung with green lamps. According to Mahmoud, all the candles were to light the imam's passage after his death.

"Is this where...?"

"Yes," he said. He pointed at the distant stage, then opened his hand and made a motion like a windshield wiper. "Tomorrow – there will be hundreds here."

"Where's Parvin?"

He frowned slightly. "Her phone is not on."

They wandered into the gridded space. It was crammed with people, mostly youth. Gas lanterns and feeble fluorescent tubes. In the half dark, fewer people stopped to notice her. The air smelled strongly of burning meat. Mahmoud behind her, she passed a cluster of stalls selling chains set in wooden handles. Then juice vendors and smoking grills. Her mouth watered; she stopped to buy kebabs and immediately a quick-witted boy accosted them, hawking popsicles. His eyes became large, almost insectoid, when he saw her face.

"I'm sorry," she murmured.

There was a stirring at the far end of the square. The sound of firecrackers and the sputtered brightening of smoke. They couldn't see anything through the crowd.

Mahmoud accepted a kebab from her but didn't eat it. They left the congested market stalls and walked into the green halo of a multi-lanterned tree. "You come to Iran – during Ashura – and do not want to talk politics?" He spoke loudly, over the square's hubbub, and his tone seemed to have risen in pitch. "Who comes to Iran if not for politics?"

She looked at him and realized he was joking. It accorded, she felt, with her beginning ease in this place, her sense of being slowly let in. She recalled what Roya had said about him being a hero. As though he'd read her mind, he turned away.

In front of them was the large stage. Actors mimed a battle scene with much shouting and clashing of wooden swords against shields. They were roundly ignored by the square's swarming youth. Parvin was nowhere in sight. Sarah sat with Mahmoud on a bench near the stage. On an opposite bench, a white-bearded old man bared his stained teeth at them. He was something sucked out from a dream. The tree behind him had flowers in it, a carpet of candles all around its trunk. As the night passed, people came and knelt and added candles in religious observance – shapes of women more fabric than human-form; men same-faced, retreating into their beard-shadows. Who were they? What were they to her? The more she looked, the less she saw of this city.

Mahmoud flung out his right arm. "You see them?" he asked. "Look."

They gathered, where he pointed, in fluid, makeshift groups. Teenagers, by the looks. Most of the girls wore high heels and flared jeans or calf-length capris. Their faces glossy and made-up. Their scarves not black but bright and diaphanous, pushed far back to expose their hair, and instead of the long, loose overgarment they wore figure-hugging trench coats that barely reached their knees. Even through her outward alertness Sarah felt self-conscious. She remembered the pilot's announcement on the plane, remembered feeling, curiously, the act of covering up as though she were stripping naked. But this. How could anyone arrest anyone at all when all this was in plain sight, was plainly permissible?

"They are not here for Ashura," spat Mahmoud. "They are here for Valentine's Day." Many of the girls were in lazy possession of bouquets and teddy bears. Couples holding hands.

"You know what they call this? 'The Hussein Party'." He didn't look at her. In the candlelight, his features seemed statuesque. He hadn't touched his kebab. She caught a sudden whiff of spice on the wind.

Firecrackers went off again, closer this time. She shifted in her seat. There ran a new restlessness through the youth. Cell phones, dozens of them, ring tones random as wind chimes.

They came from the southern edge of the park. Four cars – old sheet-metal heaps that could have been salvaged from American junkyards, one with a broken million-glinting windshield – pulled up bumper to bumper and spilled out, men with various beards, holding clubs and chains and walkie-talkies.

"It's them," hissed Mahmoud. He yanked her back down onto the bench. "They will see you."

One man swung a baton through the crowd of youth as though cutting through brush with a machete. They skittered apart. A girl screamed. Several of the men stood behind the others and spoke out through cupped hands, clearly and ecstatically. One came towards them. He paused in front of the stage and took in the show.

"Your scarf."

She pulled her scarf tight over her head, tucking in every strand of hair, leaving the front hanging, cowl-like, over her face.

More cries sounded out from the maze of stalls. The rows between them clearing fast. The men fanned deeper.

"You must stop looking at them," said Mahmoud. He moved closer to her on the bench. They were a couple now, close enough to be conventionally transgressive – but not too close. An older couple in this park of kids, with nothing to fear from these men.

Her breath caught when she saw a group of them dragging three shapes back to their cars. Then she saw. She actually felt her heart stop. The darkly stubbled face – it was Reza, seemingly unconscious. The other two were young men she didn't recognize. A strange girl stood rooted at the edge of the square and lifted her hands to either side of her nose and mouth.

"Stop looking," Mahmoud murmured. She let her face drop, inhaled sharply. Now the men were banging their clubs against steel poles. She felt each impact in the seat of her stomach. Warmth emanated from Mahmoud's body. The ground was wet, busy with candlelight, green shadows. The old man opposite started talking, roaring with laughter. Another man's voice joined in.

Mahmoud leaned in closer. "You are an American citizen," he said. "You will be safe."

"Did you see Parvin?"

"Listen to me," he whispered into her ear, "Listen to me. When Parvin first came back, she was taken."

Sarah's stomach, already riled, turned hot and sick.

"But she did not want to tell you. But she was safe. I tell you this because."

A man stopped in front of them. Bits of gravel and broken glass stuck to the rim of his soles: cheap, synthetic-leather shoes. You couldn't beat anyone with those shoes. The wooden club hanging beside them.

"*Salam.*"

"*Salam,*" Mahmoud said. Sarah kept her head bowed, the hard burl of cloth digging into her throat. The men conversed for some time. He sounded normal, in good cheer, this man with his wooden club. He told a joke and found it worth repeating again and again. Mahmoud laughed behind his words with terrible sunken sobs. Then the man fell silent – a short lull – and when he spoke again his tone had changed. He was speaking to her.

Mahmoud said something in Farsi. The man reacted animatedly, quarrelling now with the exaggerated intonation she'd come to expect, through TV, from Middle Eastern men – that windy, slightly petulant swing of voice. Mahmoud turned and murmured to her, but in Farsi. Those words – their lilting, curious energy – she was sure they held the key to her life. If she could just understand those words. The strange man reached down, elbowing Mahmoud aside, and lifted her chin.

Breath rushed into her windpipe; she started to cough, then stopped herself.

The man considered her. There was a dangerous looseness through his face; his wide-spaced eyes, his purple lips swelling out through his beard. She felt irrationally as though she already knew him, had encountered him already in some similar situation. Mahmoud so young, fresh-faced, next to him. The man said something to her. She was aware of his companions prowling the square behind him as he prodded the club into the damp ground, leaving a mesh of curved dents. She forced herself to smile – the effort tearing up her eyes – then she drooped her head again. The lamb kebab lurching up from her gut. She had to not vomit.

What choice did she have? She stood up. The man shouted aloud. Three other men rushed over, one snaking a steel-link chain behind him, another's trousers sodden at the ankles. The smell of gasoline strong off them.

Her heart pounded her skull. "I am an American citizen," she said. Her voice came out squeezed, for some reason English-accented.

They all fell silent. Then the first man laughed, a harsh, high-pitched sound. Mahmoud got to his feet, started talking, his speech gaining momentum. He took out his wallet and showed it to the man. Sarah kept her gaze trained on the ground. All four men started laughing, then at one point the man with the chain threw a question at Mahmoud. He replied. Behind them the clatter and thrum of car engines, distant human cries from the street. The square itself had gone quiet. Finally, the first man tossed back Mahmoud's wallet and lifted up his club with a twirl, like a baseball player loosening his wrist, and tapped it against the sole of one shoe, then the other, and when his second shoe met the ground he'd already swivelled and walked away. The others followed him.

Sarah waited, blood surging in her ears. Not daring to look up. Finally, she did. The square was empty. The cars were gone. They were safe.

She turned to Mahmoud. "What did you say to them?"

His face was tight, sickly-looking.

"What did you say?"

"You saw who they took?"

She nodded.

"They said they took them as American sympathizers."

"But not me."

"Not you." He chuckled dryly, "I told them you were nothing. You are a foolish tourist I guide around our city."

She shuddered her head. She felt dizzy in the green-glowing landscape. Flags snapping in the wind.

"Who were they? What will happen to Reza?"

"I said I wanted to show you this beautiful square and it is too bad, with all these infidel youth."

She clutched his arm. "Where's Parvin?" she asked. She felt a desperate compulsion to keep asking.

Mahmoud chuckled again, an abrasive sound like he was hawking up phlegm. "You are an American woman. He was jealous of me, for being with you." They both sat down. She realized she was shaking, was chill with sweat. He took out his cell phone and dialled a number. She watched the fingers of his free hand as they twitched beside his legs, as though in some mean-ingful order, as though warming up some invisible instrument. He tried another number. Another. Finally he got through. His voice swerved to a different pitch and pace. She waited – all that time, waiting – time driven into the act of waiting for him while he talked. He hung up.

"Her phone is still off. No one has seen her."

She collapsed her face into her hands with a moan.

"No one knows who was taken with Reza." He cleared his throat. "I think it was a random arrest. But we must wait. We must go somewhere safe and wait."

"Who were they?"

His face went distant. "Ansar-e Hezbollah, they call them-selves. Friends of the Party of God."

"Then why did they let us go?" She swallowed; her throat was dry. "What did you say to them?"

He shrugged. She felt it through her arm and chest and legs. "What did you say?"

He looked up at her with his dark eyes, then bowed his head. "You want to know what I said?" His jaw tensed. "It is not that I am religious or not."

"What?"

Now his voice was harsh. "I told them," he said, "I told them I was the son of my father." His expression glazed over for a moment, then he swung around to face her. "Now tell me the truth. Why did you come here?"

"What do you mean?"

He waited, his eyes coruscating in the candlelight. After a drawn-out silence she looked away.

"To escape," she said. And she laughed.

He laughed too, but bitterly. "Then you are the first American to escape to Iran."

"To escape from a man," she said. It surprised her to say it. To hear herself say it – a giddiness overcoming her and with it this urge to tell out her life, those problems so personal she could only tell them to a stranger. She looked at Mahmoud in the green-gold glow. His face drawn into the slightest suggestion of a smirk – as though it had forgotten itself in the middle of self-mockery. He'd invoked his father's name. He'd saved her from those men. He'd left her at odds with herself. There was sadness and then there was this, a field of candles, smoke-flowers in the wind.

"Parvin," he said, "she comes here to find a man." The mock-lines on his face deepening. "She says she wanted to meet me before she marries me."

"Marries you?"

"She will marry me to save me. So I can go to America if I want. If I choose."

He wasn't joking. He seemed amused by her silence.

"We are not all birds flying in the same direction. We are young – most of us are young." He rubbed his chin with the heel of his hand.

She forced herself to nod.

79

"Perhaps I will let myself be saved," he went on. "I, too, am young, and expect much from the world."

"How old are you?"

His pupils were gunmetal black. "I am twenty-three. I know what you think. You look at me and you do not see me as a man. I know."

"You're wrong."

And he was. At every turn he'd misunderstood her mind. She was thinking of Parvin; she was thinking of the man in front of her who was Parvin's betrothed, that it was yet another thing she didn't know about her best friend. She was thinking of Reza and of Zahra Kazemi and the man with fat purple lips. She was thinking of Paul. There was no incongruity at all – or maybe everything was incongruous. Maybe that was the condition of things. She was thinking of their drive here, how everything would seem like the grimy, industrial, urban standard – when suddenly she'd glimpse the yearning tapering of a spire, the delicate axis of an arch, and, for a moment, she'd remember to exist alongside the ghosts of this ancient city.

Mahmoud led her through the black streets. Many of the mourning candles now snuffed by the risen wind. Dogs roamed the alleyways. She followed him to a tall apartment building, one side of which had been whitewashed and painted over: a twenty-story portrait of a man with a gray beard and black turban. This one wearing glasses. The background was laid down in green and red, the whole wall unevenly illuminated by spotlights.

It was a different hotel. In a blocked-off alley behind them a group of men laughed raucously. A boy wearing a baseball cap urinated against the wall.

The man at the desk was angular and trim-bearded. He watched them unremittingly, not once looking away.

In the room Mahmoud went over and drew the curtains shut. "We will be safe here for now," he said.

"What will happen to Reza?" she asked again.

"I do not know." He started to say something else, then checked himself. "All we can do now is wait."

Again, her breath started coming short and fast. She gulped down some air. "But you think Parvin's okay?"

He sat beside her on the bed. "I think so," he said. Then in a smooth yet awkward gesture he wrapped his arms around her. She neither resisted nor relented.

For what seemed like hours they stayed in that room. Twice he answered his cell phone but learned nothing new. Sarah kept going to the window, lifting the curtains by their hems, looking out into the blinking night as though the act of looking might make her friend appear. Out there it seemed like any other place but underneath, she knew – she understood now – there was an alien body. A deep and adverse structure.

Seven thousand miles she'd come and she'd failed their friendship in every way. Parvin had confided in her – had made her mind and soul intelligible – and Sarah had pushed her away, pushed her into the teeth of some horrible proof. There was the thirteen-year-old girl, those small dark rooms and small bright rooms, there the woman with a girl's face, the man trussed by his wrists to a ceiling fan. A metal chair with a gas flame beneath it. Her heart smashing inside her ribs. Why had she come here? What had she wanted? She'd wanted purpose, sure, but every part of this turned-around place gave purpose to some action – leave, never leave, come back. She'd wanted to look past herself but now, when she did, she saw nothing at all that was different. She was alone. Parvin was alone.

Mahmoud was standing behind her. Then he was propping her up, sliding her closer to the bed. He laid her on her back and went away, returning with a glass of water.

"It is okay," he said. He handed her some hotel napkins. "Listen to me. She will be safe. Like last time."

"How do you know?"

"Try to rest," he answered.

She pushed herself back on the bed. The naked bulb glaring down from the ceiling. The sound of incessant traffic outside. She stilled herself, succumbed to the noise of her body – its angry clunk and shudder. After a while, Mahmoud leaned over her, looked at her closely before saying, "Wait here."

"Where are you going?" She was revolted, even before she

spoke, by the desperation she expected in her voice. She closed her eyes, started shivering. She waited.

Hours passed, or maybe minutes, and he came back in and chain-locked the door behind him. He took off his jacket. Then he laid out on the desk two long pipes, a plastic-wrapped baggie, a candle.

"This will help," he said.

"What is it?"

He looked up at her curiously. "It is better than drunk."

She knew, on some level – on the level that experienced this place as a series of unfolding stories – that there was amusement, irony, in this. She was receiving the all-Iranian experience. But two days had shattered that way of being here. What she'd thought about things no longer mattered. She was here, now.

Mahmoud fidgeted with his instruments. He struck a match, lit the candle. The pipe shifted in his mouth as he persuaded the white smoke in and out.

"Here," he said. It smelled like chocolate caramel. She watched his fingers, how he shaped the gummy resin until it was pea-shaped, worked it into the widened hollow at the end of the pipe. "Lie down like this," he said.

"Like this," she repeated.

The pipe's bum end was metal, black with an old burn, and he held it to the candle flame. A tindering sound. "Follow the smoke."

She did as he said and followed the smoke.

"Like that," he said. He was serious now, that little secret smile on his face. He didn't know her at all. He was kind. He taught her how to rotate the pipe. He prepared the other pipe. Then he gave it to her and she handed him the first and then, when they were done, they exchanged again, almost formally. His shirt tucked tight into his pants. He caught her eye and they both looked away. Much later, he talked, his words solvent with smoke. She talked too. At one point he stumbled up and turned off the light. At one point the streetlamp stopped working and after that there was only candlelight.

He put his hand between her legs. She saw it happening, the feeling arriving after the thinking about it – it was maybe mildly disagreeable, she decided. The candle flame reflected off his skin so that his cheekbones and forehead became patches of brilliant white, as though the light had burned clear through.

She closed her eyes. The floating night before her.

"How do you feel?"

He sounded far off, acoustic, calling to her as though from the bottom of a well. There was water in her now, light in her body, in her lungs. Words floating up in bubbles of air. She followed the smoke and breath by breath her body gave out its substance. She got up with the slow, easy motions of a swimmer.

She was at the window, looking out. The light-spilled streets like narrow banks, the metal stream rolling ceaselessly between them. Lights from cars, candles, distant streetlamps deranging themselves into an emptiness so bright it evaporated everything. Parvin was out there somewhere. Inside those lights. Parvin, her friend.

Mahmoud called for her from the bed.

You could never know. Streets. Women walking, wind whipping their clothes. Black chadors loose and flaring behind their bodies, shreds of shadow. Wind blowing against their faces, shaking the veils smooth as sheets on clotheslines. Lights. You could never know when the light would take on weight again and crush you. She pushed herself against the glass. She was alone, and there was time yet. From the tops of plane trees, black birds hurled themselves against the sky –thousands of them.

"Sarah!"

Her name carried, still, a remote comfort and she stopped for it.

THE FROGMAN

NIKI AGUIRRE

It was only while standing at one of the busiest airports in the country, waiting for a boyfriend she had never seen before, that the absurdity of Sam's situation began to make itself apparent. Two months back, when she first met Andres online, they'd sent one another the requisite blurry photographs. But aside from minor details – she wore glasses, he was 6'1" with sandy hair – they remained blissfully ignorant on the subject of one another's appearance.

This being the early, heady days of the internet, it was quite common for couples to fly thousands of miles without having any real clue as to what the other person looked like. Most descriptions given over chat tended to be vague, pedestrian and highly exaggerated, so at least this way there was less intentional deception and a lot more romance.

The night before Andres' flight, Sam rang and asked him to describe the exact colour of his eyes. "I mean how blue are we talking? Claudia Schiffer or Paul Newman blue?"

"Is there a difference?"

"Yes."

"Claudia Schiffer blue, then. And you?"

"Brown, Winnie the Pooh honey-brown, with tiny specks of yellow in the iris."

"I can't wait to see you," Andres whispered and Sam held the receiver closer to her chest.

★

At the airport, she checked herself critically in the bathroom mirror. She enumerated her good points; heart-shaped face, wide eyes, nice smile. And defects: chipped front tooth, shortsighted, occasionally oily skin. She hoped the positives outweighed the negatives. But what if it wasn't enough? What if she didn't possess the pattern of womanly attributes he admired? What if he tried desperately to be attracted to her and failed.

She heard them announce his flight. "This is your last chance," she said to her reflection. "You can still eject from the pilot's seat and land in relative safety. You can still leave with some dignity. Make your choice now. Risk it all or burn baby, burn." A woman washing her hands at the other sink gave her a strange look. Sam smiled and shoved her hairbrush into her bag.

Andres was a twenty-seven year old Chilean writer. He edited a small literary journal that didn't earn him much money, but within certain circles it offered him the reputation of vaulted intellectual. Sam, was twenty-one, in her last year of a teaching degree. She was taking an advanced class in Spanish and joined a chatroom in order to practice with native speakers.

Andres: Do you know many Latin American writers?
Sammie: I've read a few.
Andres: Such as?
Sammie: You want names?
Andres: Yes.
Sammie: Cortazar, Borges, Puig …
Andres: They are *Argentines.* They don't count.
Sammie: They don't?
Andres: No. Who else?
Sammie: Gabriel Garcia Marquez.
Andres: He's from Colombia. Disqualified.
Sammie: What? How can you disqualify Marquez?
Andres: Don't you know any writers from Chile?
Sammie: How about Isabel Allende or Neruda?
Andres: They doesn't count either.
Sammie: Why not? They are from Chile.
Andres: Correction. Allende was *born* in Peru. Peru is not Chile.

85

Sammie: Shouldn't matter. Plus Neruda was born there.

Andres: Sorry, he doesn't count. *Everyone* knows Neruda. He's like a bottle of Coca-Cola. People know what to expect from a Coca-Cola.

Sammie: That's ridiculous.

Andres: How about Dorfman, Donoso or Sepulveda? Do you know David Rosenmann?

Sammie: I can't say I've heard of them.

Andres: Ay, that explains it. So you read books only for your courses? Not for pleasure or for knowing something else. For curiosity for example?

Sammie: I read all the time. I just haven't gotten around to reading every obscure writer on your list.

Andres: Dorfman is not obscure!

Sammie: I was hoping we could chat about books, maybe discuss some recommendations, but you seem to want to talk only to people who can list Chilean writers at a drop of a hat. If that is the case, your elitism doesn't interest me.

Andres: You pretend you are friendly, but you are not very flexible, ay? A body is supposed to be flexible. You are too rigid. You have to be more relaxed.

Sammie: Excuse me? What does this have to do with my body? First you complain about my lack of knowledge, now you insult my body?

Andres: I meant a body like a person. Not as in your *body*, per se. I don't know what that looks like, but I think my imagination is how do you say, *aroused*. You have to forgive my English. It is not always perfect.

Sammie: Neither is your system of classification. According to my notes, Dorfman was born in Buenos Aires.

Andres: Well maybe on paper yes, but *spiritually* he is Chilean. He lived in Santiago and spent much of his life there, so he is one of us. Not Argie. But you are very observant.

Sammie: Gee thanks. Listen, I read books because I want to read them, not because it is cool or special to do so. I wish I had more time so I could try a little of everything. I may even enjoy this Dorfman of yours. Then again, I may decide he is rubbish. I don't pretend to like something only because it is the literary flavour *de jour*.

86

Andres: I understand. It is impossible to read everything. Just when you think you achieve this task, there is always a new writer or poet. Even *I* have not read all Latin American writers in their entirety. One of my professors used to say that Dorfman is the Chilean equivalent of James Joyce. All students claim to read him; but I don't know many who actually enjoy him. Better to like a book for its own sake than for the status of saying you've read it.

Sammie: Wow, look at that. We just agreed on something.

Andres: Have you ever heard the term *Cuestión de piel?*

Sammie: Not really, no.

Andres: It is a feeling you have when touching someone's skin that you can either be great friends or great lovers. It is tactile. It is explosive. It is electrical and instinctual. It is an instant awareness of endless possibilities. Virtually it also exists, *claro*. It is not only a sensation limited to the physical.

Sammie: If you are asking if I want to be friends – then YES, I would like that very much. I have a feeling that despite our different approaches, we look at things in similar ways.

Andres: Yes, I agree. I have a good feeling about this. A very good feeling.

There must have been at least 250 people on his flight and Sam eagerly scanned every one of them, even the women. What if Andres found someone else on the way to meet her? That happened to a girl she knew online, the callous guy actually approached her with the other woman in tow. She would die of embarrassment if that ever happened.

Sam watched a tall handsome man with fair hair disembark. Could this be him? He had eyes of midnight blue that were staring straight at her.

"Andres?" she said hopefully.

"Nope. My name's Chris." said the man. "Who is this Andre you are waiting on?"

"*Andres.* He's my boyfriend."

"And you don't you know what he looks like? Did you order him through a mail order catalogue? Get it? *Male.*" The man laughed uproariously at his own joke. "Well good luck finding him."

"Thanks," said Sam looking around the almost empty lounge.

A lot of her non-virtual friends found reasons to joke and tease her. They said she was pretty and outgoing. Why was she finding boyfriends over the computer? At first she tried to explain but it was always the same polite nods and smiles. They didn't understand. How could they understand? "We like one another's personalities," she'd tell them and someone without fail would respond that "good personality' was a code for hideously ugly loser who can't get a date.

"Excuse me," Sam asked a clerk. "I suppose you couldn't tell me if a certain passenger on your flight actually boarded?"

"Now you know I can't give you that information."

"I know, I know, it is just that my boyfriend. Well, I have no idea if he missed his flight. He's come a long way and I don't want him to be here, all alone. He doesn't know anyone and he doesn't speak English very well."

Something in her face must have made the clerk soften. He brought up the passenger list and said there was no mistake about it. Andres had checked onto the flight.

The only people remaining in the passenger lounge now were some crew members and a young family with a little boy who refused to unglue himself from the window.

"Todd, come away from there and we'll buy you some ice cream."

"I don't want ice cream. I want to see the planes land."

"But mommy and daddy are tired now. Let's go home and we'll see the planes another time."

"No, I want to see them now."

There was a man sitting in the row behind the family. Sam hadn't noticed before, as he had been slouched in his seat with his feet curled up underneath him. He was scowling at a magazine. Could that be him? He didn't match Andres' description. He was much too slight and his hair was dark instead of sandy. Also he was wearing blue jeans and her boyfriend claimed he only wore black.

The man looked up and Sam held her breath and counted to ten slowly. From that distance she couldn't tell the colour of his eyes, but if he looked away before she reached the end, the odds were it wasn't him. If however, he stared back with any curiosity, it meant he was also waiting for someone – maybe even her. But before she reached four he'd returned to his magazine, slouching down until he was practically invisible.

Sam wondered what to do next. Could she have missed Andres in the crowd of passengers? He probably went straight to her apartment and was waiting for her there, upset and worried she hadn't shown. As she walked toward the exit, she passed the man that wasn't Andres and noticed his hands were soft and pale, almost transparent. He didn't look up at all.

Sam recalled a conversation they'd had about work; although both her parents were lawyers, she'd always worked since the age of fifteen. She cleaned stables, worked at a summer camp, an ice cream parlour, and during university vacation she stacked books at a library.

Andres told her how much he detested the corporate world. The goal was always the same: money and more money. "Mindless occupations eat up your soul," he said, claiming he'd rather starve than sell out for a job.

"Don't worry, if you're broke you could always pawn your Dorfman books," she joked.

"Ja-ja. That would barely raise enough for a can of beans and a bottle of red wine. Art, my dear, doesn't pay in Latin America."

The decision to live together was Sam's. Andres had mostly finished his first book of poetry and could edit anywhere, really. Why not in Chicago with her, she reasoned? She had a little studio apartment big enough for the both of them and a job lined up as soon as she graduated. If it didn't work out, well, she didn't want to consider that. But there was an implied agreement between them that there were no promises and no restrictions. They were both adults and he could come and go as he pleased. He had said he always wanted to experience life in America. Now she was offering him the chance.

A few days afterwards, she visited her mother to tell her the good news.

"But you've never had a serious boyfriend, much less a live-in lover. You're very young, Samantha. How are you going to cope?"

"The way all couples do, Mom. Slowly and painfully, learn-

ing about one another. We love each other. Please try to understand."

"I can't, when you insist on making rash judgements. Do you
really know anything about this young man? Have you given
thought to the possibility that he is only using you for a visa?"

There, it was out. Others had hinted at it. Her mother was
direct enough to say it.

"Oh mom. It isn't like that. Andres isn't that kind of guy. He
doesn't really care about money or visas. He cares about writing.
Not everyone wants to come and live here in the US. Some
people like their own countries, you know."

Her mother turned back to the pie she was baking. "Are you
hundred percent certain of that? Whose idea was it for him to
come here."

"Mine. All mine. I had to talk him into it."

"Well obviously he didn't resist too much. Samantha darling,
don't let naivety blind you. Some people will do and say anything
to achieve their goals. I just don't want to see you get hurt."

"I won't mom. I love him and he loves me."

"Yes, but there is more to it than love. How will you both live
on only your salary? Will he work? How about your cultural
differences and the language? Doesn't he have a family back in
Chile that he'll miss?"

"We'll work it out. Plenty of people from different countries
get married."

"Marriage!"

"No, I didn't mean us. Not yet, at least, but who knows…
maybe in the future…"

"Oh Sammie, I'm trying to understand, but this is too much,"
said her mother, putting down her towel and walking out of the
kitchen.

Sam walked to the taxi rank. A few minutes later the man she had
previously seen in the passenger lounge, approached and got in
line. Now that they were outdoors, she could see him better. His
skin was bloated, with a greenish tinge that reminded her of a
frog. And he was short – a good two inches shorter than she was.
Oh God, this couldn't be Andres. He didn't look at all as she

imagined. His face and podgy body didn't go with his voice, which was deep and strong. This guy looked hopeless and downtrodden. The kind of person you passed on the street without a second look. No way this was Andres, she thought, trying to discreetly catch glimpses of him.

She thought back to their conversations. The promises she had made. She wasn't a shallow person.

"So many expectations of beauty and emphasis on desire," Andres had said. "It ruins what is at the heart of the individual. It destroys any relationship based on something deeper. After all those hours of conversation and sharing of ideas, why does it turn into fear and desperation? Are they that shallow? How do you think blind people fall in love?"

"Let's make a pact," Sam had said. "Let's not be one of those couples that we've heard about. They ones who claimed to be in love until they met each other face to face. Let's be like Mallia and Steven (who married six months after meeting online without ever seeing a photo of one another). Are you game?"

"Depends," Andres said. "Is this a game, or are you serious?"

"I'm not sure yet."

"I want to be able to trust you completely and I want you to trust me. In fact I promise that nothing will change the valued opinion I have of you right now. Even if you are 4' 2" and weigh 250 pounds, I will continue to like you. In fact, I take it one step further. I will not send or accept any more photographs or talk about expectations. If we are to ever meet, it will be because I am confident we love one another completely."

Sam stared at him and this time there was no mistaking it. Frogman held her look for at least 12 seconds.

"Miss, are you waiting for a cab?"

Sam quickly got in and slammed the door without another look at the frogman.

Please don't be him, please don't be him, please God, don't let that be him.

Sam was not one to get hung up on physicality, but even she had limits. So why was she reacting this way to the poor unfortunate man who just happened to resemble a limp frog? She was certain it wasn't even a question of his skin or his blank, colourless eyes but her conviction that Andres, her true love, could not possibly look that way. Although, she knew that was also silly, as it was perfectly clear now she had no idea what he looked like.

Until recently, her perception of him had been a blank slate and as soon as he told her what to expect, her mind had conjured up someone handsome, waiting like a cyber knight in tight black jeans. Ok, that was equally silly, but Frogman ruined the dream by being a very plain person who had no right to exist in her fairytale dream. If she couldn't reconcile his face and body with the man she's spent the last few months chatting with, what hope did they have of making this work? She knew by instinct that there was no way that she could ever be with this watery, pale amphibian.

But if he was really Andres why hadn't he approached her? Medium length brown hair, she told him. Brown eyes and she would be wearing … she reached up and touched her head. Oh no! She must have forgotten her hat in the airport bathroom when she was fixing her hair. She'd said he'd be able to recognise her by her beret.

Sam closed her eyes and leaned against the worn leatherette of the cab. The driver was saying something, asking for her destination, but she was too busy watching the man she was certain was definitely not Andres. Frogman was moving toward the cab, which was now peeling away from the curb. The poor man looked even more lost than before; he was dragging an enormous suitcase behind him, his bloated skin blotchy in the morning light. He shouted something and then throwing aside his case, he made a mad dash, groping onto the rear bumper. Frightened, Sam whirled around in her seat and faced the road. "Could we please hurry it up," she said to the driver. "I'm in a hurry."

She turned back only once to face him; his pale fingers still holding on to the back, although she could tell he was tiring. He attempted to mouth something she couldn't understand. The exaggerated effect of his lips moving slowly made him look even more like a sea creature. But his eyes, now that she could see them up close, were a startling shade of Claudia Schiffer blue.

MPONDO

BRIAN CHIKWAVA

"Tell me," he says, drumming the bottom of the mug with his fingers and emptying the last dregs of *Thabani* brew into his mouth. "What is this that I keep reading, that overseas, where you decided to flee to, people of your generation have brought nothing to the world but curiosity and a credit card with which to satisfy it?" He clearly still reads. Putting the mug down and sinking into his armchair, he eyes my coloured trainers. His hairless head and the short clumps of beard sprouting on his face give him the look of someone bitter and distinguished.

"Er... erm, I'm not a vacuous consumer if that's what you mean," I try to convince myself. This is my first trip back home in a while and I only decided to visit him out of concern for his situation.

He pulls his pipe out of the inner pocket of his dirt-stiffened tweed jacket, lights it and absently sucks it, only stopping when, with practised disdain, he starts laughing smoke out of his mouth. Now he stares at my watch. Calculatingly. After all these years, his eyes have lost none of their glare. Back in the years when boarding school was still rough, when some of the senior boys were fist-trading ex-guerrillas – and local whores were regularly hurled out of dormitory windows, the sight of Mpondo, billowing great clouds of smoke and duck-footing down the pathways, was the only thing that, without fail, brought deferential whispers and the disappearance of all signs of ill discipline. Mpondo, the boys called him – short for *mpondo kayitshintshwa*: never ever change a pound note into coins – the archetypal, iron-fisted Ndebele patriarchy's supreme edict, to be dutifully adhered to by the spendthrift woman of the house until a directive to the contrary was issued.

"I wasn't talking about you, young man," he says, blowing smoke.

We eyeball each other; we say nothing to each other. My eyes wander. So this is what his life has come down to. Compared to the other lodgers' rooms, his was spacious, he said. Six by eight pig-thief's steps, is how he described its dimensions. At ceiling level a length of string was tied across the room, from which hung sheets of *The Chronicle* newspaper, stapled together to cover the entire height of the room, creating a wall and two separate spaces. One room is the kitchen, long and narrow, the other his bedroom and study – slightly bigger. We are in his bedroom and study; I, sitting on a tall pile of books leaning against the wall and he, on his armchair, behind a tiny desk.

"Can I get some water?"

"Help yourself young man. There's cold water in the fridge."

"How do I get out?" I say, unable to pick the door out of the newspaper wall.

"Down there; page 27. Page 27, young man. That page, you can roll all the way up to the ceiling."

I push through the composite sheet and it gives way.

The fridge, taking up most of the kitchen floor, is a tall old machine, occasionally coughing and rattling but not quite shaking its rusty door off the hinges. It could easily take a whole cow. Nothing inside except for a topless 2-litre bottle of water and frozen blood stains presumably from meat. There being neither cup nor glass in sight, I take the bottle of water with me.

Page 25 to come into the room. This is the sheet that carries obituaries. At face level, and turned at right angle anticlockwise, a black and white picture of Mr. Guma stares back at me with cold wild eyes. He was once our chemistry teacher.

"Thirsty," I say, sitting on the pile of books and lifting the bottle to my mouth.

"It's good eh?"

I nod, the bottle fixed to my mouth.

Now he busies himself picking bricks of bank notes from the floor and arranging them on the table. There are supposed to be eighteen of them – $18 million. All of them from me. I'd said: "Forgive me, I know this is tacky, but I didn't have time to get you tobacco on my way and hope you don't mind me giving you money." This was how I had got myself out of a hole when charitably placing a £10 note on his desk had elicited a withering look. Having decided that tobacco money was acceptable, he sent me out to go and change it into Zimbabwean dollars. The old woman who sold vegetables, reed baskets and small bags at the street corner offered the best rate, yielding $20 million but I couldn't carry it all without a sack or large bag.

"Get one of these bags. $2 million only," she pointed.

"$2 million for this little bag?"

"My son," she said, embarrassed, scratching the dusty ground and avoiding eye contact, "that little bag can stretch and stretch for ever; it's made from manhood skin."

I bought it without further query.

"Did she count it correctly," I say, putting the bottle down.

"Yea yea. Yea this is what our independence means; this is our sovereignty," he says, his voice rising and falling with sarcasm. He eyes the many bricks of notes piled up on his tiny desk, rubs his nose thoughtfully, sucks his pipe and stares at his old academic robe that hangs on the opposite wall, its arms tattered like a bullet-riddled imperial regimental flag. His passion was rumoured to be Charles Dickens, but no one could be sure; being the school head, he never took classes.

"Next week I get my monthly pension payment. $4,145. That was a lot of money a few years ago," he says, throwing his head back and looking up at the ceiling. "And when my dear Ellen passed and left me alone, I didn't know what to do with all this money in that first year. Now you can't even buy a thief's fart with $4,145. Yes, what have you young people brought to the table except curiosity, bank cards, weak spines, weaker minds and an even weaker sense of civic duty? Does anybody else in this country feel the way I do?" He sits upright now, stabbing the air with his chin for emphasis. "Never mind me, my dear boy," he says retreating into a more avuncular persona now. I say nothing.

"What happened to Mr. Guma?"

"Why you ask?"

"Er, I saw his obituary there." I point.

"Ah that." He looks up at the ceiling. The corrugated zinc roof sheets are audibly crackling as they cool down. It's evening.

"Mr Guma – he died of foolishness."

I wait for him to elaborate.

"You remember those villages to the west of the school?"

"Yes."

"That's what killed him. That and foolishness. Arrogance. He thought himself a chemistry genius; thought himself a better being, disrespected the villagers and yet loved their brew. That never works." Mpondo sucks his pipe again. "Aggrieved villagers have their own ways of putting you in your place. They poisoned his beer; he drank, he died and they scattered off to their fields and carried on hoeing as if nothing had happened."

A coughing fit seizes Mpondo.

"Doctors say I should be dead."

Hanging on the return wall, above his single bed, are five pictures. Another one of Mr. Guma is at the centre of them.

"Those were my best teachers," Mpondo says with regret. Above the pictures, a Ndebele warrior's knobkerrie and a spear are fixed to the wall at angles in cross formation. A small hand-axe hangs carelessly on a nail beside a white cow's tail.

"What happened to these other teachers? Mr. Ngulube?"

"They all died of foolishness of one kind or another. Who can ever figure it out?" he says, eyes bloodshot and challenging. "They were good people, though. They visited me here. Perhaps to say goodbye." This time his face is softer and less quarrelsome. He looks tired now.

Outside, at the gate, a vehicle screeches to a halt, promptly followed by a high-spirited exchange between the man who has just driven in and the wife of the next door lodger.

"Them. They are also doing it. Meat. No one knows where it comes from and no one asks. It is always delivered way into the night. Three a.m. sometimes. Who can blame them? People have to survive. Even I also need to survive." He sucks his teeth, skews his jaw to the right and lets his tongue run over his front teeth, under sealed lips.

I glance at my watch. It's 7.33pm.

"We have to survive. Who can blame us?" Mpondo says, not paying attention to me.

"Now, come with me," he says standing up. Evidently relaxed, he now breathes out through an orifice of common ill repute, pushing our relationship further into unfamiliar territory. He starts to put the money back onto the little bag; it stretches painfully with each brick of notes he shoves in.

"Right!" he says, his task complete. He picks up his pipe again and shuffles to his bed. He puts one foot on it, then the other, and stands there swaying unsteadily as the bed springs creak. He throws one foot forward; the next step throws him towards the wall, which he holds onto with both hands. Shaking. With one hand, he plucks the axe off the wall and quickly comes down.

"Right! Follow me, young man." He picks the bag off his desk and leads the way out. Page 27.

"She too," Mpondo points accusingly, as we drive past the old woman who changed the money and sold me the little bag. She cuts a lonely figure under a now lit sodium street lamp. "Where do you think she gets her things from?" Not wanting to distract him while he's driving, I say nothing. My God you still have this old car, I nearly say. He's had it for decades – a long and wide 60s Chevrolet Impala. It is clearly his only remaining luxury now.

"And the neighbours across the road – their son disappeared without trace and suddenly they bought two cars. Some kind of meat, they say, can bring prosperity."

We veer madly off the road and coast into the deserted local service station. Mpondo, energetic now, leaps out and duck-foots to the kiosk. When we drove off from his lodgings, a few curious and ghostly long faces eerily poked through curtains. Now I don't want to be left out of the loop of local whispers so I get out of the car and follow him.

"A pint of oil."

The lanky attendant has his hands reassuringly clenched together on the counter; a finger twitches and his eyes shift uncomfortably as he turns to the shelf behind him.

"How much?" Mpondo says, his eyes turning to a shabby price list sellotaped to the side of the kiosk hatch.

"$2 million," the attendant says, placing the can on the counter.

"But here it says $100 for a pint."

"Ah, those prices, they are years out of date."

"So they are all wrong?" Mpondo says, retrieving a pen from his pocket.

"Yes," the man agrees, baffled. The redundancy of the price list confirmed, Mpondo embarks on vandalism of a scholarly kind; pointedly crossing out all the old prices with his pen, the paper getting torn to bits by the pressure he is applying.

"Now the new prices – $2 million for this one, you said. Next; brake fluid – how much is that then?" he demands, pointing his chin at the puzzled attendant.

"Forgive me, so what did you say you are doing now?" The Impala is now brain jigglingly swerving across lanes, avoiding pot holes and heading for the outskirts of the city.

"I write."

"Ah, of course,' Mpondo says perfunctorily. "What do you write?"

"Fiction."

"What kind?"

"Er, good fiction." My mind is elsewhere. As yet I have no idea where we are heading, but I don't want to seem unduly paranoid.

"Good fiction?" Mpondo breaks into scornful laughter. Maniacal laughter. "What do you think is good fiction, young man? What is good literature? There is no such thing, you should know by now. The greatness of a work of literature is not just a matter of the writer's genius; it's also dependent on the contents of the mind of its reader. Throw a single drop of water into a beaker of acid and the reaction can be explosive; but what does a drop of acid do to a beaker full of water, tell me? Hardly noticeable." The car swerves again. My hands are moist and Mpondo is frantically scratching his chin.

"Where are we going?"

"Oh these bloody lice; they won't leave me alone. Plenty of lice eggs I find in my beard everyday."

"Where are we going?" I ask again as soon as he gets both hands on the steering wheel.

"Now, have you got a picture to leave behind with me when you go back? A young writer like you must have lots of pictures, no?"

"Right now, no."

"What a shame."

We turn off into a gravel road.

"So, do you think you will come with me to church tomorrow then?"

"No, I won't be able to." I am getting resentful at being roped into things.

"Don't worry, I know you won't be able to."

"Are you still a member of the Seventh Day Adventist Church?"

"Of course."

"Still not eating pork and other unclean food?" I say, sarcastic for the first time. At this, he stops talking.

They all shall sweetly obey thy will, he starts whistling. I recognise the refrain – a hymn we used to sing at school:

Master, the tempest is raging! The billows are tossing high!
The sky is o'ershadowed with blackness. No shelter or help is nigh.
Carest thou not that we perish? How canst thou lie asleep
When each moment so madly is threat'ning a grave in the angry deep?
The winds and the waves shall obey thy will…

"That's an Anglican hymn?"

"Wrong!' he says dismissively. "More likely to be Presbyterian. You still find it at many state schools. There used to be lots of Scots in this country, young man. But then again it could be American; I'm not sure. Oh I don't know these things; I'm just a village boy who grew up breaking oxen in Ntabazinduna."

"Where are we going?"

"I have at least to get some use out of you that belong to a useless generation. Tonight's my only chance," he says and starts whistling. *They all shall sweetly obey thy will, peace be still peace be still…*

Mpondo pulls off the road, still whistling absently. The moon shines deathly silver.

"Right!" He jumps out, goes to the back of the car and returns with his axe.

"Now follow me, young man," he says, jumping into a road-side ditch and taking a path into the thick undergrowth. There are lights shining from a few sparsely scattered houses around us – about a kilometre from each other.

I get out of the car and follow him.

"What are you walking slowly for?" he growls, waiting for me as I make my way towards him, twigs crackling under my feet.

"How strong are you?" he says as I catch up with him.

"Very," I answer emphatically.

"Good. We shall see." He prods my ribs with the handle of his axe, motioning me to start walking in front of him.

"I don't know where we are going."

"Just follow the path, foolish young man." The moon shines on his face, his beard now a scattering of silver splotches – the silver of the wings of green-bottle flies.

I hesitate, take a step forward, stop and turn around.

"Keep walking." He prods impatiently with his axe handle. I walk.

"You have been here before, obviously," I say, throwing a glance behind.

They all shall sweetly obey thy will, peace be still peace be still, he whistles with cultivated carelessness.

We walk. Interminably, it seems. Aimlessly, it seems. Each moment hatches like his lice eggs, takes off on silver wings into the night, discharging its small possibilities into the darkness. Later, when all has amassed into a singularly clear probability, I shall come tearing through the vegetation, out of breath, back to the gravel road, Mpondo wheezing way behind me.

I will jump straight onto the driver's seat, the car keys still dangling in the ignition. The car, though, will not start. My fingers still slippery from blood, I will crank the ignition again. One more time. Nothing. By now Mpondo will be just a few steps away. Still with his axe. Before he just prodded me with it; then he will use it to shove me clean off the driver's seat and I will roll over. A single turn of the key and the vehicle will roar to life.

"Ha ha ha ha!" Mpondo laughs crazily as we speed off, leaving a cloud of moonlit dust in our wake. "I would rather be caught by our disinterested police than by our ordinary citizens. Once a whole neighbourhood of small-plot farmers, their labourers and the close relatives they keep in their shacks – those failed school graduates, local thieves and the perennially unemployable – once they wake up in all their bitter glory to find you already apprehended and tied to a lamp post as an exhibit, then ho ho ho, there is little question of you not paying for the other dozen thieves who managed to elude them. Not to mention paying for their frustrations and self-hatred for failing to properly assume their civic and moral duties and arrest the slide in this nation's fortunes. They take it all out on you, can you believe it. They will all die of foolishness. Fools."

I check the road behind us – no sign of a pursuing vehicle.

"What a shame to have to leave that creature behind. A few months of not having to worry about where to find my next portion of meat. That's the trouble it would have saved me."

I flex my leg. My trousers are wet; I can feel the blood pulsing out of the gash on my shin. That's where one of the kicks landed. All is still vivid on my mind. With the animal's hind legs in my firm grip, Mpondo swung the axe. It struck the back of the pig's head and the terrified creature squealed, thrashed, kicked about and broke free. I landed on my backside. Then it started racing blindly in the dark with the axe still stuck in its head; running into walls and making piercingly distressing noises. That's when lights lit up inside the farm house and two men appeared at the front door. But Mpondo would not leave without his axe.

"I paid $11 million for that axe. I was not going to give it away just like that," he says now. I don't answer but roll my trouser leg up.

"You are not as strong as you make out, young man."
I take my shoe off.
They all shall sweetly obey thy will, peace be still, peace be still.

A MATTER OF POSITION

NAOMI ALDERMAN

I find myself missing Hendon. Not the synagogue, or our old house, or my parents, or even the *mikveh*, not anything normal. I find myself missing, for example, the pound shop opposite Bell Lane, near the butcher, what was it called? With its rows of anonymously-branded washing-up liquid, and cheap plastic toys and a "luxury fondue set" gathering dust on a high shelf. Or I'll wake up in the night – I spend half my nights awake now, being kicked from the inside – and find that I am longing for ratty old Queen's Park, by Hendon Central Station, for its flatness and its lack of trees and the mottled yellow grass.

And I know, I do know, what this is. It's not like I haven't done it before, the last month of waiting with its fears and delusions, its hot heavy ache, it's not like I don't know the drill. And mostly I wake Saul up and he rubs my feet or strokes my belly or helps me into the shower; the baby likes the shower, I imagine, just as we like being warm inside when it's raining outside. But sometimes I can't bear to wake him and then I lie in the dark and think of the filling station on Finchley Lane, or the path behind the library towards the doctor's clinic with its cracked paving stones like broken teeth, or the new one-way system around Alexandra Road, wondering why I want them. Hendon is not a lovely place.

I try to tell Saul about this longing, this missing, but he has learned not to take too seriously anything I say in the last month. I was the same way with Avrami and Chayale and Ruti. Once, in the last month with Avrami, I began to long so strongly for my parents' house in Golders Green that he agreed to take me back there. I slept, for one night, in the narrow single bed of my childhood with my husband on a mattress on the floor by my side, a strong and ardent lion. One night, and the craving was cured. Perhaps if I could return to Hendon for one night, the longings would be gone. But it is far away, and they do not advise women to fly in their last month.

The mornings are all a swirl of excitement. The children must be woken and washed and dressed and fed and sent to school or *gan*. Saul stays late to help me with them, now that I am so big and tired. He walks Ruti to the *gan* at the end of our road, her stout little legs trotting alongside his long ones, although some of the children here walk to nursery by themselves when they are only a little older than her. The peace of this place is unexpected, considering. That was what impressed me first of all, when we were newly married and came to visit my sister's house. I woke in the heat of the morning and from the window I could see the moisture rising from the earth, and there were little children walking fearlessly and quite alone and men returning from morning prayer. A hoopoe called out softly "hou hou hou", and one of the children shouted to another "Mikael!", and although this was probably the other boy's name I could not help hearing the three separate Hebrew words that make up the name. *Mi ka el*? Who is like God? It is almost paradise here.

After the children have left for school and we have cleaned up the kitchen, Saul kisses the top of my head and rubs my back and drives to work. I shower again. It is late August and the days become hot. The fold of skin under my belly is sore from sweat and chafing; it is a pleasure to let the cool water play on it. The baby, too, likes the sensation. Inside me, he wriggles and sticks out an elbow – I can see the joint through my skin. It must be tight inside there now, little room for manoeuvre. I let him stick out his arm without trying to coax it back in.

I dry myself carefully, and put cooling powder under my stomach. I make sure that the fabric of my cotton underpants rests in the skin fold – this helps with the chafing – and get dressed. I could stay at home all day if I wanted to; the women at the shop have told me they could manage without me, and we do not need the money. But I'd get restless, spending the morning entirely by myself. I'm like my mother; we like to be busy. So I pull on my cotton dress and waddle down to the bus stop. The bus is waiting for me; it is only a local bus, making the rounds of the various villages in this area and the driver, knows I always travel at this time. If I had gone into labour, word would have got around. He knows to wait. I pay my fare – four shekels – and settle into a seat one space behind the two soldiers. Outside the settlement, the ride is bumpy and the baby protests, kicking and struggling. But in less than 10 minutes we are there.

The baby is the wrong way up. They told me this the last time I visited the hospital. At first the doctor spoke in Hebrew, and my Hebrew is quite acceptable really, of quite a high standard but when they began to talk of my baby I found my comprehension slipped away. The doctor and her assistant exchanged a glance.

"You would prefer," she said, in heavily accented tones, "you would prefer we speak in English?"

Something stubborn in me wanted to protest, to say that I'd studied Hebrew all my life for just such a moment as this. But instead I spoke gratefully.

"Yes, thank you. *Todah raba*."

"Your baby, it is, how do say this…?" she held her hands, right above left, palms facing each other, a baby shaped space in between them. Then she quickly rotated her hands, keeping the same distance between them, moving left above right. "Britch? A britch birth? The wrong way around."

I must have shown my alarm on my face. She relaxed her hands, disappearing the imaginary baby and touched my arm.

"It is not serious, we can deliver like this if we need to. But sometimes they turn around in the last month. Don't worry," she patted my arm again, "don't worry."

"*Marcolet!*" the driver shouts, and I pull myself to my feet. We are, indeed, at the grocery store – the biggest one in these five villages. One of the soldiers swings his gun behind his back to help me clamber out of the bus. He looks a little uncertain as he offers his arm; religious women often refuse to touch men, but I'm grateful

105

for the help. We were never extremists in Hendon. There's no reason to start now. I waddle to the shop door anticipating already the cool blast of the air-conditioner. It's too hot here now to stay outside for long.

The morning rush at the Marcolet is over by the time I arrive. The owner, Sharona, and her fulltime assistant Dafna like to sit in the back room and have a snack – sheep's milk cheese and ripe sweet tomatoes like we never got in England – while I tend the store. It's never such a busy time, 10am till lunch. A steady stream of mothers, young and old, once their children or husbands have been packed off to school or work. I take phonecalls from customers with accounts who are making orders to pick up later in the day. Or I sit on my sturdy chair by the register, a pillow pressed into the small of my back for support, and ring up purchases. Three crusty rolls and a package of sliced turkey for Giveret Unterman, from Russia, whose only son is serving in the IDF; she and her husband talk loudly and often of his bravery. A candy bar and a bag of crisps for the soldier who stands, rifle in hand, at the centre of the square, looking this way and that. "You should have something healthy," I chide in Hebrew, "an apple!" He smiles, but doesn't take one. A full basket of canned goods, courgettes and onions for Giveret Baum, whose family are over from Australia, visiting. She wipes her hand across her forehead in mock-exhaustion "Blahdy great having them to stay," she says, "but I have to leave the house just to get some peace and quiet!". The whole Jewish family of the world is here in our little cluster of villages.

There's a lull at around 11.45am, and it's then I think of Hendon most of all. When it's quiet. I find myself thinking of B Kosher, on the corner of Alexandra Road, of ragged linoleum and clean, orderly shelves. Of the products there from all the corners of the Jewish world, the Telma and the Osem and the Yarden which were shipped all the way to Hendon from here. Here I am, surrounded by Jewish shops, and kosher products, and Jewish people, and I find myself unable to stop thinking about that world we left because it wasn't Jewish enough. Because we hated the fear and the prejudice and the constant constant need for explanation. "Why do you eat like this? Why do you dress like this? Why do you act like this?" Here, there's no need to explain. Everyone knows their role.

At half past twelve, pandemonium. The school around the corner spews forth its pupils. My children will be picked up by a neighbour; I work here until 2pm, when the rush is over, and then collect them from her and take them home. It's hard to keep up with demand for the next hour, though. Sharona and Dafna take up their positions at the different registers and we attempt to keep a little order among the crowds of schoolchildren, workers from the offices around the square, working women trying to get their shopping done in their lunch breaks.

The children all want candy, of course. Grubby hands thrust into the basket of half-shekel treats. Bubblegum! Lollipops! Jelly worms! They push and wriggle, trying to get to the front of the queue. There's no sense in trying to make them line up; no one here knows how to queue. I look up. At the other side of the store, Dafna is behind the deli counter, trying to make up sandwich rolls fast enough to keep pace with demand. We only serve non-meat goods at the deli counter: tuna salad and smoked salmon, cheese and pickles and falafel balls, houmous and techina, pepper salad and sliced onion rings. It's a good kosher place, and if you want a fresh-made sandwich it's the only place on the square. And it's then, looking up at her, standing by the fresh-baked loaves of bread from the bakery in the next village, that I think I notice something. Something. It's a…

"Three packets of Bissli please!" shouts a small boy in front of me. I look down at him, then back up. What was it that I…?

"Two onion and one barbeque flavour!" He's shouting even though I can hear him perfectly well. I reach behind me to take down the packets of snacks. But I know that something's not right. I look back to Dafna. She's not looking at the crowd, her head is down, a few wisps of soft blonde hair escaped from her hair net framing her face. But something… there are too many people, but…

"*Atzor!*" shouts the soldier from the square. My heart races. The world slows. And it's then that, through the gap between two people, I see him.

He's not a boy, not yet a man. Maybe 18? Sweating. Not a man I've seen before. His expression is peaceful but his eyes are panicked, darting here and there. He looks like one of us except not quite, not quite. He's wearing a baseball cap, a red sweater, a pair of blue jeans, trainers. There's something bulky at his waist and there's something heavy at his waist and there's something underneath his sweater at his waist and his hand is reaching to his waistband and oh god I know, I know what's happening I know it.

And all I can think of is the baby at that moment, the baby inside me. The baby turned the wrong way round, with his bottom where his head should be and me here and not in Hendon where we have pound shops and scrubby grass and no beauty and no sacredness but not this either. And I think will this baby live to turn itself into its proper position, and will I see Hendon again, and these thoughts strike me as so ludicrous and so ridiculous that in that elongated moment I almost start to laugh.

And the man is reaching for his waist and it seems to me that every eye in the world is on him, every single one and all the fear of all the people in the world is concentrated into one glance. And I look and see that he, too, is shaking and his mouth is open and he is speaking silent words with moving lips. And he is so young, I see, so very very young; no one who was not young would be here like this. And I wonder whether I should pray too but I cannot think of the words of any prayers at all.

There is a bang. It is so loud that I feel it in the base of my spine all the way up to the centre of my forehead.

The man crumples. He is facing away from me so I do not see the side of his head, the side without the neat bullet hole, the side that is not so neat. He falls to the ground and the wall behind him, and

Dafna's apron, and the glass food guard are red. The soldier is at the door with his weapon still raised. And there is no sound at all.

The baby kicks and kicks and will not stop, and on the wall behind me, the telephone rings. I answer it mechanically, through force of habit.

"Marcolet?"

"Oh hiii, Miri, it's Sara here, Giveret Tennenbaum. Listen, can you hold three of your beautiful granary loaves for me? I'm not going to get in till 4pm and I know they sometimes go, can you put three by for me?"

I look over at Dafna, in whom the scream is just beginning to build. I look at the loaves. They are spattered with blood, every one. Every single loaf, bloodsmeared. The walls and the floor and the glass of the counter and the people standing by.

"Miri?" says the voice on the phone. "Miri?"

A RAINLESS PLACE

AAMER HUSSEIN
[From *The Cloud Messenger* (forthcoming 2011)]

1.

My father and my two older sisters shared memories of a distant place they'd lived in once. They'd talk for hours about Hyde Park and Stanmore, Selfridges and Bill and Ben the Flowerpot Men and Noddy, crumpets, and strawberries with cream. It was, to us, insufferably exotic (though we didn't know the word). At the same time their talk made my younger sister and I feel excluded, and even provincial. We lived in Karachi, a hot city, where we ate oranges, banana, mangoes, papaya and custard apples, only knew the oases and the sea, couldn't understand what strawberries or crumpets tasted like, and, lactose-intolerant, hated cream. And if my mother decided to join the others to remember that winter day when she'd walked on a pond sheathed in thin ice and fallen in, we'd feel even more excluded. Since our only picture of snow was what we saw on Christmas cards – in a place that hardly knew rain – snow was as alien to us as chimneys and Santa Claus.

Our father received the *Times*, in gauzy sheets, every two or three days, and he'd discuss ballets and pantomimes with my sisters: one of their most vivid recollections was of being taken to see Russian dancers perform *Swan Lake* at the Royal Opera. (For us, entertainment, in those times without television, meant films, puppet shows, amateur theatricals, fancy dress parties and fairs.) Father also had letters from abroad with pictures of the Queen on their stamps. "Does she rule us, then?" we'd want to know. "No," my mother said, irate. "Why," we'd ask, "do we call her a queen?" "She's the Queen of England," we were told.

Was England in London? Was London in Pakistan? Or in India? We knew India was far away, because getting there required a drive to the airport, a wait in a lounge, a trip on a noisy plane, and a much, much longer drive into town once we reached Bombay.

No, it isn't, it's much further than India, very far away. On that at least we could agree.

We saw the Queen in 1960, I think, when I was about five. She wore a yellow-petalled hat and waved to hundreds of bystanders from a car. My English sisters were taken to meet her; we weren't. As I remember, I didn't mind; I'd be taken to meet Sirikit of Thailand and Zhou Enlai of China in years to follow, and would feel quite silly garlanding the latter and his wife on the steps of a plane. In England, our mother was taken for a princess (which she was, in a way, though she didn't like to be called that) – or a movie star. (One day, she came across Louis Jourdan shooting for a film with Leslie Caron. She asked them for an autograph; they took out their pens and asked for hers). At home, she seemed quite normal, though she was different from most people's mothers. People often gasped at her beauty when they saw her; she sang very well, and frequently drove her little car up one-way streets.

My oldest sister had every Enid Blyton book that had ever been published, and inevitably we read them as we made the transition from picture books to more grown-up tales of adventure. But though I couldn't understand the food they talked about – marmite and potted shrimps – their picnics seemed very adventurous in comparison to our sedate family outings when adults and children drove off together to the seaside or some green place. Then, the thrill of their midnight feasts was something we couldn't replicate; getting up to raid the fridge after midnight seemed an exceedingly tame act when the fridge was stocked especially for us with apples and pears and chocolates and cheeses, and some hapless servant might rise and rush to ask us what we needed, thinking we'd been underfed at dinner.

But though the Famous Five made our life seem unadventurous, reading about England made me no more curious than I was about China or Estonia. The first foreign city I visited, at Christmas when I was nearly eleven, was Rome, which I had wanted to see. When the chance came at the end of that Italian trip to visit London or Beirut, I preferred to go to Beirut because it was on our way home and I'd heard London's temperature was below freezing. But Andersen and the Brothers Grimm and the narratives in the Old Testament and the Koran I loved until and beyond the time I graduated to the *Iliad* and the *Odyssey* and Plutarch's *Lives*, and later, courtesy of my sisters, Shakespeare and Tennyson and Wilde and Shaw. Recently, I questioned a friend from Karachi who said her vision of the world had been shaped by reading Enid Blyton and other British children's books. "How," I asked, "when our mental landscape was so different, could we feel inspired by the exploits of Dick or George or Fatty?" "Blyton made me curious about other places," she said, and I could recognise that instinct, but my curiosity about the world was sharpened by those headier texts I read when I was older.

Again, without knowing the word, I knew when I was about five that my father was a permanent expatriate. Born in Karachi, he'd grown up in many other places and, as a teenager he'd gone alone to England where he studied for several years, until in 1939 his father's anxieties about the war took him away. Ever since, one of his regular residences has been a plane. And though he was very much a part of Karachi – it was hard to imagine the city without him, and when he was away on one of his very frequent trips, the space of his absence was larger than his presence, to be filled only by the extravagant gifts we knew he'd bring – he was always dreaming of other places.

I am evoking my father with a lot of words that begin with exes – exotic places, exclusive memories, extravagant gifts – but the only one of these ex-words he shared with my mother was expatriation. My mother was more immersed in my father's native city than he ever seemed to be. Apart from getting us to school on time, often driving or collecting us herself, then overseeing our homework, there were charities, art exhibitions, fashion shows, diplomatic receptions and concerts. Or, at home, the music lessons twice a week, or the occasional article she was bullied into writing by my aunt or some importunate friend who worked for *Dawn* or *The Morning News*, that kept her busy from morning till, at times, after midnight, writing by hand and then dictating over the phone. Then there were the huge family gatherings we hosted occasionally on Sundays, when all my father's cousins turned up for enormous meals.

It was rare for our mother to leave Karachi without all of us in tow. Her expatriation was of another sort. We knew she'd moved here as a bride in 1948, gone with my father soon after to London, and when she'd come back a couple of years before I was born – I understand this now – she'd made every effort to recreate a semblance of the landscape she'd left behind. An early memory of the first house we moved to in the late '50s is of a truck arriving to plant grass in our barren yard – I may be inventing this, but I'm sure that they chose the house because it was on a hill full of hedges and wild flowering bushes, with soil more fertile than the sand and rock that seemed to make up most of Karachi. And when, one day, I said that I remember that the garden grew lavishly green overnight, my father laughed. I wasn't far from wrong; my mother tells me today that the grass – imported, she thinks, from New Zealand – was of the fast-growing sort.

Try as she did, our mother's Karachi gardens could only create illusions of her native place: the air and the water were different. What we had was a case of artifice triumphant, making more beauty, perhaps, than the abundance nature allows. She had grown up in a region where vegetation was lush, trees very tall, and there were wells and running water at every corner. So the gardens she made combined natural resources – bougainvillea, cactus, frangipani, guava – with imported orchids and roses. The search for home was more a question of green motifs: grassy beds and shadowy places. In 1961 she moved us higher up the hill, to a house in which another expatriate had made a garden with terraces, arbours and bowers, and almonds and stunted orange trees in great coral-coloured pots that probably evoked the greener places she'd left behind.

My sisters, with their Anglophile ways, were on the other hand participants in a very local noise and glamour. They reached their teens in the new house, in '62 and '63 respectively, and studied in the international milieu of the Convent of Jesus and Mary, where I, too, was sent at the age of eight. Two or three times a year they'd have parties in the garden to which all their school friends, foreign or local, came dressed and made up to kill, and danced till their cars came to take them home at the Cinderella hour. They inhabited some private city within the city, their own particular teenaged fairground.

But to my mother the topography of sandy, stony Karachi, with its tall palm trees and stunted cacti, felt foreign: we were always tacitly aware of that. Of all her children, I at least inherited something of her estrangement from the city's climate. And all her children longed for rain, as if we were born into intimacy with the rainy season, though we'd grown up in this rainless place: many of our games involved sprinklers, fountains, tubs and ponds to create illusions of the monsoon. Once, when I was three or four, there was a three-day downpour and the watermelon patch filled up like a pool, and – with our mother – we bathed in its tea-coloured water. It must have been in May. Sometimes, though, on summer days when the heat was overpowering, or dust storms forced the city to shut down for the space of an afternoon, or clouds promised rain for three days at a time and never delivered a drop, our mother would admit she was missing her childhood home. We'd plead with her to make plans for our next journey.

2.

The places she'd take us to we could share with her; unlike London, they were three cities we knew well, the only otherwhere we had, and more exciting to us than unknown England or Enid Blyton. There was Bombay, that big, messy city which, like ours, was by the sea, but couldn't be more different in every other way. It grew upwards, and was hemmed in by its waters, whereas in Karachi houses were houses, smallish and detached and enclosed in walled gardens, and the sea was miles and miles away from where we lived. Bombay was entertaining. My mother's sister lived there: her son was two years older than I was and, in spite of differences of character, he would, for many years, remain the closest surrogate I would ever have to a brother. You could see the sea from all the windows of their second floor flat. My mother's childhood friend lived only a few minutes' drive away with her daughters, whom we loved as if they were of our blood, though we didn't even share a religion. They were in glamorous Marine Drive, on the face of the sea.

More built up than our city, Bombay had cinemas a few moments' drive away from New Cuffe Parade where we stayed, and a club by a beach even closer to our block of flats; shopping for things modish or traditional was an hourly event. In Karachi, by contrast, we lived in fast-growing PECHS, a half-hour's drive away from the centre of town; getting to the cinema or the sea side was a long haul, and there was only a little market called the Nursery a short walk away from us at the foot of the hill, where everything from marzipan cakes to paperback novels, from sanitary towels to sticky toffees and sharpeners with wiggly 3-D figures on them could be had. There was an ice cream parlour called Dew Drop Inn frequented by the more louche teenagers of the area, whom we knew as Teddies, in their skintight clothes; we could only drop in if we were in adult company, otherwise we'd have to send the driver in to buy us strawberry ice cream cones. No such strictures in Bombay, where cones could be had on every corner. It was as if we had strayed from a still and enclosed world into movement and expansion. Bombay people were louder and freer and more gaudy than we were, and also – at least, in comparison with our privileged class – spoke less elegant English, saw Hollywood movies and heard British pop later than we did (the Beatles, the Stones, and Sandy Shaw were more in vogue with us all then, in the mid-sixties, than American singers); they still wore drainpipes when we'd migrated to flares.

But mother was always impatient to move on from Bombay.

Another city we knew well was Gwalior, where my mother's sister lived. Family weddings seemed to happen frequently here, as her daughters married and left, one by one, and her son brought his bride to take their place. You couldn't imagine a town less similar to Karachi. The Gwalior house was an old white

115

mansion with at least four courtyards, inner and outer, winding staircases, galleries and hidden passageways, surrounded by a babbling street busy with three-wheeled cabs, horsedrawn carriages, and rickshaws. We had to switch languages here, practising our Urdu grown threadbare with disuse, with various members of the extended clan who would have found our English chatter a frivolous affectation. The city was surrounded by forest, ravines and rivers. Hunting duck and deer was a frequent pastime with women and men alike. (In her teens, my mother shot a crocodile; her older sister bagged a tiger.) There, we seemed to have gone back in time to the graciousness, the contingent rules and regulations of an era of *noblesse oblige* which, with all its sometimes welcome strangeness, had always been familiar from our parents' ways. But if, in Karachi, we'd tried to tell friends about riding elephants on wedding days, or shooting deer in bandit-infested forests, they'd have thought it all not only exotic but far more unbelievable than Enid Blyton.

Then there was the town my mother missed most of all: Indore, her home town, which I mention last because it remains, to me at least, if not to all of us, the most important. There, the passage to another time was complete, but this, rather than calendar time, was the time of fiction, though I only recognised this in my thirties when I became a voracious reader of Urdu novels. To the children we were, it was a story that we were living rather than reading, living and also writing to read later, as if it were a diary, when we were back at home.

My grandfather, the patriarch, had his domain on the ground floor, which was at once drawing room, study and library, where books from east and west sat side by side: *Annals and Antiquities of Rajputana* next to Hawthorne, Fitzgerald's Khayyam elbowing Plutarch and an Urdu translation of Firdausi. He also had a room upstairs, overlooking the garden, in which he spent time until an injection left him – that man who'd walked several miles a day – unable to walk without great effort. His den was the central room in the front wing of the ground floor, which led into the garden. To its left, if you faced it from the inner courtyard, was my grandmother's realm. She held court from her four-poster bed, with her books and a few treasured objects beside her. Not averse to certain western innovations if she found them comfortable, she had opted for tradition in her own room. The fine carpet on the floor was always covered by a crisp white sheet, littered with fat cushions, on which her children, grandchildren and guests sat around her. The only foreign intrusion in this room was the easy chair, close to the always open door, that she kept there for my grandfather's frequent incursions into her kingdom. (Once, she said she was taking her afternoon nap when she thought he entered and sat down, and lit a cigarette; she smelt the smoke of perfumed tobacco linger in the air. She didn't hear him leave. A little later, awake now, she saw him come in again. She apologised for not having roused herself before. I wasn't here, he said. Another incident, also in the afternoon, took place when in her sleep she felt his hand play with her silver anklet, and opened her eyes to find no one there.)

In the courtyard was a room that stood apart, like a little pavilion, which was occupied by my grandmother's sister, another wanderer who moved from town to town depending on the season. She was a widow, and the clan's storyteller. Fiction or fact, you could rely on her to keep the records, or straighten the twist in the tale. Among the romances she told over three afternoon sessions – she always stopped before sunset – were "The Prince with the Needles in his Eyes", and "The Patient Princess". (My older sister, a writer, would later develop and indulge a passion for collecting and retelling such tales.)

To the left of Grandfather's domain was my uncle's apartment, a little bastion of modernity within the timelessness of his family home. Furnished practically and smartly, it was remarkable, above all, for the range and number of books in it: in the bedroom, novels by Nabokov, Murdoch and Barth; in the study, volumes of Indian history, where I read enough about ancient and medieval times to get a high mark in an exam, without studying the set texts, when I was thirteen, and had then relocated to a school which, though in India, was so far away in the South that it seemed to be in another country.

My uncle, like another of his brothers who lived far away in the southern mountains and came home for summer and winter holidays, had chosen to be a teacher. He had three children, two girls and a boy. His oldest daughter was closest to my grand-mother. Very tall with light brown hair that fell to her hips, her footsteps and her shadow seemed so essential to the corridors, courtyards and gardens of the house that when, in 1968 at the age of eighteen, she left to marry our aunt's son in Gwalior, it seemed that, like my aunts before her, she'd take something away. Instead, she took something of Indore with her to her aunt's house, interlocking even more tightly the destiny of two houses and two families.

In some ways, life in Bombay and Gwalior resembled each other: drives, shops and the cinema, and always a lot of food. But the pace of Bombay was faster, and everywhere you had the sense of the city and the sea surrounding you; in Gwalior, the houses we visited were bigger, and often in quiet, leafy places, near rivers or lakes or hunting grounds. An endless cavalcade of guests and invitations was reminiscent of Karachi, but in Karachi you could have the occasional empty day too: not here.

In Indore, life's pace was tranquil, and for a city child restorative. You read, ate fresh fruit from the garden and honey from a farm on some family member's estate. Occasionally you drove to the centre of town. It was there that I discovered, at the age of nine, the numerous translations of Indian classics, the *Ramayana* and Kalidasa's plays and poems among them, that you could buy in cheap local editions from a bookshop called Rupayana, near the India Coffee House where, after your book-shopping, you could regale yourself on crisp dosa washed down with hot South Indian coffee. The neighbour's son, Kapil, who taught me to ride a bicycle and took me to see Hindi films on warm afternoons, remained my best friend for ten years, though I only ever saw him for two or three weeks a year, and would almost forget him when I went away. But every year he'd be there, in the courtyard, on his bicycle, calling out; and I would go down, take my seat behind him, and he would whizz us down the lanes into the centre of town. (Years later, something I said about life in a quiet place amazed a friend whose family was from Indore: "It's a bustling big town," she protested, "not at all the sleepy place you remember").

In Gwalior, too, there was a bookshop – Sahitya Sadan – where you could buy Indian books. Here there were cheap editions of nineteenth-century French novels as well as Indian classics: Zola's Nana or France's Thais lowered at you from under curtains of blonde hair, looking like Diana Dors or Belinda Lee in fancy dress. I think I bought my first copy of *The Decline and Fall of the Roman Empire* – an abridged edition – there. Such books nudged works by everyone from Sartre and Moravia to Pearl S. Buck and Marie Corelli and living Indian authors such as Manohar Malgonkar and K.A. Abbas on my aunt's bookshelves.

3.

I learnt to read randomly in Gwalior in 1964, carrying home an adult reading habit which my Karachi aunt, my father's sister, indulged by giving me *My Cousin Rachel* and *Gone With the Wind* when I was ten – the latter causing me to wake up at night in panic, thinking the Yankees were coming, especially when, later that year, war broke out between India and Pakistan. That season, my mother, who'd tried to inculcate a taste for Dickens and the Bronte sisters in us, bought me a handsome edition of *War and Peace*: better an epic than a pot-boiler, and a racist one at that, she must have thought.

The Karachi aunt lived next door to us. Widowed young, she'd reinvented herself as a member of parliament, travelled frequently to attend its sessions, and remarried a man who lived in Pindi and visited her rarely. The arrangement seemed to suit her very solitary ways. When she was at home, she lived alone with a cocker spaniel and two parrots, all given to her by our father. Her library had everything in it – in expensive hardcover – from Isak Dinesen and Iris Murdoch to Flaubert and Pasternak (chosen, my sisters were convinced, by the Book of the Month Club). I was summoned into her presence to share her supper of soup, grilled meat and two vegetables, followed by fruit or creamy confections; I was rewarded with a book or two to take away for a week. She ran a glossy women's magazine which, at various times over about a decade, was managed by my mother and my two older sisters. We were taught to give her unstinting affection, since she had no children, and it took me years to realise how very little she had given any of us in return.

"When did you first miss Karachi?" my mother asked me not so long ago. "Not Karachi, but the idea of a city of my own," was my unpremeditated answer. It was long, long after leaving, when I'd spent half my life away, that I began to excavate a city sunken in my depths. The house and garden in Indore, on the other hand, and even the landscape of Gwalior, had always stayed in my consciousness. (When, in 1981, I'd revisited Bombay after a ten-year absence, it was as if I'd never left the place or the people there.) I do remember, at nine, on a trip through Bombay, waiting to go back home while the rain was relentless and my mother was lingering; I knew it was late August, my father had taken my elder sisters home before their new term began, and the time had come for us to go. Was it my books I missed, or our house and garden? One or two friends, or the way I knew the city centre well enough to guide a driver anywhere I needed to go alone, most frequently to a bookshop? (I knew the artery of roads and byroads around Elphinstone Street, Saddar and Bunder Road, all the cinemas and sweetshops and vendors of fruit and food, and was, under my father's expert tutelage, a seasoned shopper.)

But Karachi, which had given me my sense of city life, was never my only place; perhaps because of that I always felt slightly restless there. Was this, perhaps, a question of the city's rainless climate? Or the nine months I spent, cramped in my aunt's guest room, already an unwelcome guest in the city I should have called my own, while my mother struggled to stay on in what she felt was her children's hometown and encountered only resistance from many members of my father's clan, particularly his younger and most beloved brother? When my sisters and I left her there alone, before my thirteenth birthday, to join my father, it may have been to see whether we'd be happier, at least for a while, in our other monsoon world. For years I never looked over my shoulder at the city I had left behind. Karachi in the 70s and 80s remained a foreign place to me. When I went back for twenty days I was forty-one, and almost a stranger. I didn't contact most of my father's relatives, though the one aunt I did visit forced me to meet some of them. (A Nicosia-born friend of mine, when I told her that I felt more at ease today in Delhi than in my native city, said: "I feel that way about Istanbul. I'm definitely Cypriot, not Turkish, and you certainly seem more Pakistani than Indian. You and are I easiest, I think, in places that let us feel at home but lay no claim to us." Perhaps she's right. But I'd slightly rephrase her words. I'm at my ease, too, in places that lay partial claim to me.)

So what did I miss about Karachi in those years I never thought about it? Did I miss my father's Westernised, English-speaking relatives, with their Cambridge degrees and garrulous ways? We lived separate lives, in different, distant parts of town, they in Clifton, Bath Island and Defence, we in PECHS. Apart from those family Sundays, the two big Eids were the major occasions for the extended clan to get together. That was when we saw the relatives we referred to as "The Sindhi Cousins", who were gaudier, bawdier, and far more loving than the Karachi clan, with a gift for feasting and a love of music which meant that they invited some renowned singer to perform at every festivity. In Karachi, worship seemed tied to the cycles of the day and the calendar: you prayed when you saw the new moon, which announced the coming of Ramadan and of Eid, as the rising of the light announced the time to commit yourself to the day's fast, and the setting of the sun announced the time to break it with another prayer. So there was, in my mind at least, a connection between the sky and the seasons and God, Who remained an exterior and primordial being. I remember only one Eid in Indore which, apart from a visit to the mosque for the men and special sweets, was as quiet as any other day. My grandmother prayed, without any ceremony, five times a day, as did most of my mother's people. Looking back, I have come to see that prayer there had ceased to be a ritual to become, instead, reflection, an intense and private duty which brought your Maker closer to you than your jugular vein. Now, in London, I often read the prayers I do in daylight, in a room where leaves press against the glass through which I can sometimes see clouds reflected, while I am still contained within the silence of walls and windows.

In Karachi, every rhythm of the day was broken by the telephone. There was a telephone in Gwalior, too, but because people came and went without announcing themselves it wasn't often used: I do remember my aunt, though, interrupted in a Mahjong game, calling out to me: It's for you. (I'd been called by Nina, a girl my aunt didn't really like, probably to arrange an outing to the cinema.) I was about to turn fifteen, and I didn't know that I'd never see Gwalior, that girl or my aunt again. (And what is the loss of a place compared to the grief of losing people? Grandfather, grandmother, aunt, cousin – I took an interminable journey that severed me from all of them. It was only when my grandmother died that India called me back in a voice so loud I had to listen. As it calls me back, time after time. But let me count the ones I saw again, in London or in India – aunt, uncles, cousins, friends – to console me for the ones I lost.)

There wasn't a telephone in Indore. You read and you talked and you listened to stories and played in the garden and in the cool of the night you went for after-dinner walks along the leafy lanes. Then, refreshed, you left. I never felt I'd have enough of this life until, in my fifteenth year, I stayed there for two months, and started to long for cityness again. It was as if I were shedding, cell by cell, my reason for belonging. By then I'd spent eighteen months in that small town in the Southern hills, and tasted the salt of foreign cities – Rome, Naples and Beirut; I'd left behind my birthplace for ever, and already knew I'd soon be moving on, to live in the rainy city my father and sisters had made their own so many years before, the city I had never seen.

CHRISTMAS IN KITGUM

MONICA ARAC DE NYEKO

Santa knew she would leave Kitgum one day. She just did not know when. All she knew was that when that day came, she would rise and walk the fourteen miles from Mucwini to the Bus Park in Kitgum town. She would carry nothing with her except her headscarf, a baby shawl and her daughter on her back. She would have no husband. She would remember nothing.

She left Kitgum on a Thursday.

There were few travellers when she arrived at Kitgum Bus Park. The touts who usually scouted the long asphalt road on the highway were already there, shouting and calling to passengers to enter the three empty buses: Horizon, Northern Leg and Covmo Express. The buses were all gearing up for Kampala, the city where there are more people than grains of salt and Acoli is not the only language spoken.

Of the three Kampala buses, Covmo was the second in the bus queue that day. Santa took that one. In between three numbers, the even number was best. It was the number of luck. But Covmo did not stand for luck only that day. It was much more than that. It was the colour of sand, the kind that you found at the bank of a river. It was always wet, damp. Cupped in a hand, it did not crumble. It stayed there like hope. It stayed there stamped like a footprint.

One hour, maybe two after Santa sat in Covmo, the bus was ready to leave. There were one hundred and twelve passengers. They filled all the seats. Some sat on the floor. Others stood up holding onto the metal rails of the bus ceiling. Most of the ssengers were women, smalltown traders. They smelled of fish, unwashed knickers and sweat. In the bus were school children too. At this time in their lives, there was no greater adversary than the Uganda Certificate of Education examinations. In the bus were also extension government workers, trekking to far-flung counties to reassure farmers that the price of cotton would rise, that ginneries would be rebuilt, cooperative societies would be formed. Their job was to tell people that the government had a lot of plans in the works for them. The plans were as numerous as the words of the Acoli language itself.

Covmo scuttled on the Marram Road out of Kitgum town with its passengers. Unlike the other buses, which flew on the roads like kites, Covmo drivers were trained to deliver their passengers on a one hundred and twenty kilometres per hour speed, nothing more, nothing less. Too much speed was bad. The Kitgum Road could be unkind. During the rainy season, it filled with mud. For weeks mud sunk clogged car tyres. It choked the road and made it impossible. In the dry season, the sun scorched hard. It burrowed into the ground and burnt it bare. For months, encouraged by the dry winds from Sudan it dug deep into the soil until the road was nothing but gullies and trenches.

On that Thursday when Santa travelled, the dry season was just stirring. The road was good. It allowed Covmo to navigate its contours. Covmo traversed the Marram, alternating between the left and right, bouncing its passengers up and down, making them hold onto the bus seats for balance, bump their foreheads on the metal rail and slap their hands into the windows in annoyance. Outside, Covmo made straight for bicycle riders with sacks full of groundnuts. The bus surprised them, lifted them off their seats and tossed them flat on their backs to curse at it, their heads scratched by the roadside flowers and shrubs. Covmo left pedestrians choking with dust, children waving in excitement, drunkards clapping at the awe of such innovation, such a vehicle. Covmo left Kitgum as if it would never return. It did not look back at Hilltop – Kitgum's raised rock hill from where tiled houses looked down at the town. It did not look back at the Mission Hospital where people got malaria tablets for a small fee. It did not look back at the market whose shopkeepers enjoyed listening to its comings and goings. Most of the shopkeepers at the market just opposite the bus park had been there for years – before Covmo, before the Akuyon night club and before the welding workshop on the road leading out of the town. Over the years, the shopkeepers had adapted Covmo into their routine, into their lives, into their rituals. They waited for it to depart each morning and then they waited for it to return like a lost relation.

That Thursday, they watched Covmo depart with Santa in it. Santa did not notice the shopkeepers but her daughter did. She waved and smiled before sinking into her mother's bosom to chuckle. Santa covered her face with her palm and thought about Covmo. She had never used it before. When she sat in it, she did not know what to expect. All she hoped for was a safe journey to Kampala where ghosts mingle among the living and conmen flow like the city's traffic. Santa hoped for too little. Covmo offered her more. It collapsed eight hours of travel, over three hundred kilometres, into three episodes of sleep. During those episodes, Covmo painted her dreams the colour of sand. The journey became as short as a thumb.

Santa was not awake when Covmo slowed down to make its way through Murchison waterfalls. She did not see the elephant that blocked the bus's way when they were crossing the park, or the baboons, which sat obligingly as the passengers took pictures of them. But Santa was awake when the bus crossed into Kampala for the remaining forty kilometres of the journey. She lifted her head up and stretched her body. Her daughter was awake too. She had not cried; she had not stirred. Santa looked at her, held her up by the armpits. Santa showed her the city, pointing at people and buildings with the motion of her fingers. No words were uttered between mother and child, but both looked into the eyes of the city which was now theirs. They thought that there were many people in the city, very many people. It was not December, not Christmas, but the city was festive, colourful, full of life, full of haste.

Covmo arrived in Kampala at three in the afternoon. Santa located her travelling bag. She lifted her hand to wave at the bus turnboy. The boy, who could not have been more than fifteen, smiled often. He waved back. Santa thought he would make a fine husband one day – if only he found another job, did not meet many strange women and did not have to stand next to the bus looking lost and bored. The boy walked away from Covmo, which was now dusty and more brown than sand. Tonight or maybe tomorrow, he would turn his face towards the north, and start his journey all over again.

Buganda Bus Park, where Covmo parked, was in the centre of Kampala. It sat right in the belly of a valley. It was sandwiched between Mengo, Namirembe and the not too distant Makerere Hill. It was especially close to the Old Taxi Park where Santa was headed. From the Old Taxi Park she would try to find her way to Kasenke; a place she knew nothing of, except that many people from Kitgum started from there.

Santa walked the quarter kilometre from Buganda Bus Park to the Old Taxi Park. The Old Taxi Park was filled with everything but it was especially filled with taxis, mini buses licensed to carry fourteen passengers. There were hawkers, dust, noise, Orbit gum wrappings, fruit peels, and paper bags. Everything was in abundance. Even the shops offering food were many. Usually, when there was too much, Santa relied on her right hand. The right hand was always right. It gave her clarity, showed her the way. The way was always to the right.

At the Old Taxi Park, Santa turned to her right. There in the distance was a food shop. What it was, really, was a shop with several plastic chairs, tables and table mats with fruit motifs – Mama Tina's Hot Hot. Despite the small paths and hurried people, it was not difficult for Santa to make her way among the taxis, merchandise and hawkers. A minute or two later, Santa stood by the doorway of Mama Tina's Hot Hot. It was painted sand, with a green door and a sisal doormat. Santa put her hand to her chest. She slid her fingers into her brassiere. She took out the green note and walked inside. She stood in the line of people queuing for food. She held her money in her right hand. The note was the one with the picture of a man. He had a hoe. He held it at almost a ninety degree angle. The man's legs were apart. His shorts were tailored. They were firm on his body. His hair was short and tidy. There was no hair on his face. No excess in his expression. No ambiguity in his posture. There were banana trees in the background. Their leaves stood straight against t blowing wind, never swaying, never bending to any tide, not even death. The bananas looked stiff on the note.

It came Santa's turn to be served. She had seen the prices crafted on the white walls in oily blue ink. She stood before the food woman, maybe she was Mama Tina or maybe she was not – either way, the woman was seated on a stool with several saucepans of hot hot meat, hot hot cabbage, hot hot posho, hot hot rice and hot hot matooke. As soon as the Santa stood before her, the woman took out a plate.

"Fry and posho?"

"Meat and pilaou," Santa said.

The woman did not lift her eyes to look at Santa's face. She did not notice her hair was plaited with thick black Seagull threads woven on each chunk like ropes. She did not notice Santa's teeth biting into her lower lip. She did not notice that Santa's lips were dry, that it was a hot day and the sun stood upon the Old Taxi Park like a watchman. The sun peered its rays into thoughts like needles.

The food woman extended her hand to Santa. She wanted the note with the picture of a man before she would give her the plate of food. Santa handed her the money. She handed over her restless visitor, whose departure was always inevitable, whose journey was endless, whose thrill was in freedom, shifting and movement forward, to the next hand, to the next shop, to the next man – it was a whore.

The woman gave Santa the plate.

"Thank you," Santa said.

She moved to sit on the bench. Santa sat to eat at three thirty that afternoon of the year she left her husband, taking her daughter and nothing else. Hours after she left Kitgum, Santa sat in a food shop in Kampala. She ate meat. She chewed the rubbery pieces in her mouth. It tasted like the unknown – bland, hard and blurry.

Time is a chariot rider. It is as fast as a car, as stealthy as a fart.

It has been eleven Christmases since Santa came to Kampala.

daughter, is now a big girl. She is in her last year of ▢ool. She has no breasts, only nipples. She has a tongue ▢ away at heavy words with the ease of a panga in a ▢tion. She has no fear. Labolo has the audacity of a girl with breasts the size of coconuts. Her mother worries about her. She asks too many questions.

"Why don't we go to Kitgum for Christmas?" This is her question when December arrives and Kampala starts to empty of its people. In December people abandon the city. They return to the places of their birth to sit at warm fireplaces, eat maize, sing carols and tell tales about Kampala and its ghosts. During Christmas, no one except the forgotten stay.

"Why don't we go to Kitgum for Christmas?"

Santa's answers are always the same.

"We shall go to Kitgum next year if our father in heaven wills it."

Many times, Labolo has thought about their father in heaven. He is the father whose name is God. He is the God whose name her mother spells with a big G because she prays to him every morning, every night and every Sunday. The God of Santa is the one who Santa has believed in and is sure is able, as the song says:

But I know whom I have believed,
And am persuaded that He is able
To keep that which I've committed
Unto Him against that day.

Labolo's god, however, is not the same god. This is how she imagines him. This is how she has created him: a God who will not let her go home to Kitgum for Christmas is a small god. His name is spelt with a small g. He is a sad god. His tears drizzle on a sunny day and hail at dusk. When Labolo looks in the sky (which she does often), she sees him standing over her head with a bowl. He is in the blue and white clouds, in the air shaking his head and saying: no Christmas, not this time. This god in heaven above is not her father; if he was, she would know, she would feel it. She does not feel it. So she knows. And because she knows, she cannot stop asking questions. She cannot stop seeking.

Time is a chariot rider. It is as fast as a car. As stealthy as a fart. Time is like Kampala. Kampala is like time. But Kampala is not a single thing. It is many things. Kampala is a virgin by day and a whore by night – available, determined, anxious. Kampala is you in January – festive, drunk, horny. Kampala is the future – uncertain, large, promising. Kampala is wealth – temporary, excitable, fluid. Kampala is a prisoner, a prisoner sentenced to death by hanging – waiting, wishing, making amends. Kampala is Santa – a woman unravelling like a bandage. Kampala is silence. Kampala is Labolo. It is she who wants to go to Kitgum for Christmas because Christmas in Kampala is not Christmas at all.

Because the god with the small g has refused to let her go home for Christmas, Labolo has decided to stop expecting it. Instead, she has turned to numbers. She searches for answers in the pages of her math books. As her teacher once said, in math there is the answer to everything. Any problem you have, there is a solution in numbers. Labolo loves math. She does not have to cram and try to remember with math. The formulae and numbers just multiply, divide, subtract and add inside her head. Her name is written and underlined on her math book. Labolo's name is Norah Labolo.

Labolo's math book has no dog-ears. Its pages are white. Labolo uses a ruler from her mathematics set to mark out a straight margin and an additional two lines in the middle of each page like the teacher showed them. Her math teacher speaks softly. He is almost shy. He never flogs anyone for breaking the momentum of a correct probability or surface area formula – formulae he chants to them day after day like a jingle.

Surface Area of a Cube $= 6a^2$

Surface Area of a Rectangular Prism $= 2ab + 2bc + 2ac$

Surface Area of a Sphere $= 4\pi r^2$

Surface Area of a Cylinder $= 2\pi r^2 + 2\pi rh$

When she studies math, Labolo bites her fingers. Somehow the certainty of the numbers gives her this urge to nibble, nibble and nibble at her nails to the point of infinity. At the end of every school day, as she makes her way home through the Old Taxi Park, her head plays with numbers. In the chaos and bustle of activity, Labolo calculates sums. In her head, everything falls in its place. She sorts out the future like stones from rice; everything is clear in her head. For example, if Santa's father in heaven will not will their return, then she, Labolo, will make it happen. If two plus two makes four then one day she must decide that it is time to go. Labolo does not know when that time will actually be; all she knows is that when the time comes, she will take the bus to Kitgum, even if it is not Christmas.

Five o'clock in the evening of the day she turns twelve, Labolo leaves the gates of her school. She walks down to the Old Taxi Park. She makes her way to a taxi for Kasenke. This is what she does every day – goes home. So that day, like all other days, Labolo sits in the hot, humid and noisy taxi supposed to take her home. She listens to the sound of the taxi park. She recites sums in her head. Then the thought is there in her head.

"Today. Today."

The month is October, the day is Friday.

Labolo rises up. She lets herself out of the taxi to Kasenke, where she and her mother have lived all these years. Labolo rests her green school bag on her back. She makes her way to Buganda Bus Park in her maroon school uniform. There is a Covmo night-bus filling up. Labolo does not have any money in her school bag. But if three plus three makes six, then she knows she will make it home to Kitgum. It will be like Christmas.

Labolo sits in the Covmo bus and waits for it to fill up. She wants to stop counting; she cannot. There is excitement in her head. Everything is bursting with colours. These colours are as certain as math equations. There is yellow: the women selling roasted groundnuts, sesame, soya beans, Orbit and Big G chewing gum or Sportsman cigarettes in the woven baskets have wrapped many yellow lesus on their waists. There is red: the tea-sellers serve tea in big Tumpeco mugs to tired taxi drivers, panty and fruit retailers. The sellers walk around with big kettles steaming with smoke and blue aprons. They have white polyester caps on their heads and they click fifty and one hundred shillings coins in their pockets. Labolo smiles. In her head everything is bright. She does not feel the pinch of her black Bata shoes. Everything is lovely.

The evening of the Friday when Labolo takes the *Covmo* bus

130

to Kitgum, Santa returns from work early. Her daughter is not home yet. No one has to tell her this. Labolo is not coming home. She has gone home before their father in heaven has willed it. If Santa had not cultivated calm in herself all these years, she would have hurried to the Bus Park after her daughter. But Santa has learnt many things. One of these things is how to wait.

As Covmo leaves Kampala to take Labolo to Kitgum, Santa takes her stool outside and sits on her veranda.

Santa thinks of the scent of sweat and the man who left a little bird by the roadside. Her back was on the grass. Her hands were on her face. There were no tears in her eyes. That man, the one who smelt of smoke, got up and left. He took Christmas with him.

INVIERNO

JUNOT DÍAZ

From the top of Westminister, our main strip, you could see the thinnest sliver of ocean cresting the horizon to the east. My father had been shown that sight – the management showed everyone – but as he drove us in from JFK he didn't stop to point it out. The ocean might have made us feel better, considering what else there was to see. London Terrace itself was a mess; half the buildings still needed their wiring and in the evening light these structures sprawled about the landscape like ships of brick that had run aground. Mud followed gravel everywhere and the grass, planted late in fall, poked out of the snow in dead tufts.

Each building has its own laundry room, Papi said; Mami looked vaguely out of the snout of her parka and nodded. That's wonderful, she said. I was watching the snow sift over itself and the brother was cracking his knuckles. This was our first day in the States. The world has frozen solid.

Our apartment seemed huge to us. Rafa and I had a room to ourselves and the kitchen, with its refrigerator and stove, was about the size of our house on Sumner Welles. We didn't stop shivering until Papi set the apartment temperature to about eighty. Beads of water gathered on the windows like bees and we had to wipe the glass to see outside. Rafa and I were stylish in our new clothes and we wanted out, but Papi told us to take off our boots and our parkas. He sat us down in front of the television, his arms lean and surprisingly hairy right up to the short-cut sleeves. He had just shown us how to flush the toilets, run the sinks, and start the shower.

This isn't a slum, Papi began. I want you to treat everything around you with respect. I don't want you throwing any of your garbage on the floor or the street. I don't want you going to the bathroom in the bushes.

Rafa nudged me. In Santo Domingo I'd pissed everywhere, and the first time Papi had seen me in action, whizzing on a street corner, on the night of his triumphant return, he had said, What are you doing?

Decent people live around here and that's how we're going to live. You're Americans now. He had his Chivas Regal bottle on his knee.

After waiting a few seconds to show that yes, I'd digested everything he'd said, I asked, Can we go out now?

Why don't you help me unpack? Mami suggested. Her hands were very still; usually they were fussing with a piece of paper, a sleeve, or each other.

We'll just be out for a little while, I said. I got up and pulled on my boots. Had I known my father even a little I might not have turned my back on him. But I didn't know him; he'd spent the last five years in the States working and we'd spent the last five years in Santos Domingo waiting. He grabbed my ear and wrenched me back on to the couch. He did not look happy.

You'll go out when I tell you you're ready. I don't want either of you getting lost or getting hurt out there. You don't know this place.

I looked over at Rafa, who sat quietly in front of the TV. Back on the island, the two of us had taken guaguas clear across the Capital by ourselves. I looked up at Papi, his narrow face still unfamiliar. Don't you eye me, he said.

Mami stood up. You kids might as well give me a hand.

I didn't move. On the TV the newscasters were making small, flat noises at each other.

Since we weren't allowed out of the house – it's too cold, Papi said – we mostly sat in front of the TV or stared out at the snow those first days. Mami cleaned everything about ten times and made us some damn elaborate lunches.

Pretty early on Mami decided that watching TV was beneficial; you could learn English from it. She saw our young minds as bright, spiky sunflowers in need of light, and arranged us as close to the TV as possible to maximize our exposure. We watched the news, sitcoms, cartoons, *Tarzan*, *Flash Gordon*, *Jonny Quest*, *Herculoids*, *Sesame Street* – eight, nine hours of TV a day, but it was *Sesame Street* that give us our best lessons. Each word my brother and I learned we passed between ourselves, repeating over and over, and when Mami asked us to show her how to say it, we shook our heads and said, Don't worry about it.

Just tell me, she said, and when we pronounced the words slowly, forming huge, lazy soap-bubbles of sound, she never could duplicate them. Her lips seemed to tug apart even the simplest constructions. That sounds horrible, I said.

What do you know about English? she asked.

At dinner she'd try her English out on Papi, but he just poked at his pernil, which was not my mother's best dish.

I can't understand a word you're saying, he said one night. Mami had cooked rice with squid. It's best if I take care of the English.

How do you expect me to learn?

You don't have to learn, he said. Besides, the average woman can't learn English.

Oh?

It's a difficult language to master, he said, first in Spanish and then in English.

Mami didn't say another word. In the morning, as soon as Papi was out of the apartment, Mami turned on the TV and put us in front of it. The apartment was always cold in the morning and leaving our beds was a serious torment.

It's too early, we said.

It's like school, she suggested

No, it's not, we said. We were used to going to school at noon.

You two complain too much. She would stand behind us and when I turned around she would be mouthing the words we were learning, trying to make sense of them.

Even Papi's early-morning noises were strange to me. I lay in bed, listening to him stumbling around the bathroom, like he was drunk or something. I didn't know what he did for Reynold's Aluminium, but he had a lot of uniforms in his closet, all filthy with machine oil.

I had expected a different father, one about seven feet tall with enough money to buy our entire barrio, but this one was average height, with an average face. He'd come to our house in Santos Domingo in a busted-up taxi and the fits he had brought us were small things – toy guns and tops – that we were too old for, that we broke right away. Even though he hugged us and took us out to dinner on the Malecón – our first meat in years – I didn't know what to make of him. A father is a hard thing to get to know.

Those first weeks in the States, Papi spent a great deal of his home-time downstairs with his books or in front of the TV. He said little to us that wasn't disciplinary, which didn't surprise us. We'd seen other dads in action, understood that part of the drill.

What he got on me about the most was my shoelaces, Papi had a thing with shoelaces. I didn't know how to tie them properly, and when I put together a rather formidable knot, Papi would bend down and pull it apart with one tug. At least you have a future as a magician, Rafa said, but this was serious. Rafa showed me how, and I said, Fine, and had no problems in front of him, but when Papi was breathing down my neck, his hand on a belt, I couldn't perform; I looked at my father like my laces where live wires he wanted me to touch together.

I met some dumb men in the Guardia, Papi said, but every single one of them could tie his motherfucking shoes. He looked over at Mami. Why can't he?

These were not the sort of questions that had answers. She looked down, studied the veins that threaded the back of her hands. For a second Papi's watery turtle-eyes met mine. Don't you look at me, he said.

Even on days I managed a halfway decent retard knot, as Rafa called them, Papi still had my hair to go on about. While Rafa's hair was straight and dark and glided through a comb like a Caribbean grandparent's dream, my hair still had enough of the African to condemn me to endless combings and out-of-this-world haircuts.

My mother cut our hair every month, but this time when she put me in the chair my father told her not to bother.

Only one thing will take care of that, he said. Yunior, go get dressed.

Rafa followed me into my bedroom and watched while I buttoned my shirt. His mouth was tight. I started to feel anxious. What's your problem? I said.

Nothing.

Then stop watching me. When I got to my shoes, he tied them for me. At the door my father looked down and said, You're getting better.

I knew where the van was parked but I went the other way just to catch a glimpse of the neighbourhood. Papi didn't notice my defection until I had rounded the corner, and when he growled my name I hurried back, but I had already seen the fields and the children on the snow.

I sat in the front seat. He popped a tape of Jonny Ventura into the player and took us out smoothly to Route 9. The snow lay in dirty piles on the side of the road. There can't be anything worse than old snow, he said. It's nice while it falls but once it gets to the ground it just causes trouble.

Are there accidents?

Not with me driving.

The cat-tails on the banks of the Raritan were stiff and the colour of sand, and when we crossed the river, Papi said, I work in the next town.

We were in Perth Amboy for the services of a real talent, a Puerto Rican barber named Rubio who knew just what to do with the pelo malo. He put two or three creams on my head and had me sit with the foam awhile; after his wife rinsed me off he studied my head in the mirror, tugged at my hair, rubbed an oil into it, and finally sighed.

It's better to shave it all off, Papi said.

I have some other things that might work.

Papi looked at his watch. Shave it.

All right, Rubio said. I watched the clippers plough through my hair, watched my scalp appear, tender and defenceless. One of the old men in the waiting area snorted and held his paper higher. When he was finished Rubio massaged talcum power on

136

my neck. Now you look guapo, he said. He handed me a stick of gum, which would go right to my brother.

Well? Papi asked. I nodded. As soon as we were outside the cold clamped down on my head like a slab of wet dirt.

We drove back in silence. An oil tanker was pulling into port on the Raritan and I wondered how easy it would be for me to slip aboard and disappear.

Do you like negras? my father asked.

I turned my head to look at the women we had just passed. I turned back and realized that he was waiting for an answer, that he wanted to know, and while I wanted to blurt that I didn't like girls in any denomination, I said instead, Oh yes, and he smiled.

They're beautiful, he said, and lit a cigarette. They'll take care of you better than anyone.

Rafa laughed when he saw me. You look like a big thumb.

Dios mío, Mami said, turning me around.

It looks good, Papi said.

And the cold's going to make him sick.

Papi put his cold palm on my head. He likes it fine, he said.

Papi worked a long fifty-hour week and on his days off he expected quiet, but my brother and I had too much energy to be quiet; we didn't think anything of using our sofas for trampolines at nine in the morning, while Papi was asleep. In our old barrio we were accustomed to folks shocking the streets with merengue twenty-four hours a day. Our upstairs neighbours, who them-selves fought like trolls over everything, would stomp down on us. Will you two please shut up? and then Papi would come out of his room, his shorts unbuttoned and say, What did I tell you? How many times have I told you to keep it quiet? He was free with his smacks and we spent whole afternoons on Punishment Row –our bedroom– where we had to lie on our beds and not get off, because if he burst in and caught us at the window, staring out at the beautiful snow, he would pull our ears and smack us, and then we would have to kneel in the corner for a few hours. If we messed that up, joking around or cheating, he would force us to kneel down on the cutting side of a coconut grater, and only when we were bleeding and whimpering would he let us up.

Now you'll be quiet, he'd say, satisfied, and we'd lay in bed, our knees burning with iodine, and wait for him to go to work so we could put our hands against the cold glass.

We watched the neighbourhood children building snowmen and igloos, having snowball fights. I told my brother about the field I'd seen, vast in my memory, but he just shrugged. A brother and sister lived across in apartment four, and when they were out we would wave to them. They waved to us and motioned for us to come out but we shook our heads. We can't.

The brother shrugged, and tugged his sister out to where the other children were, with their shovels and their long, snow-encrusted scarves. She seemed to like Rafa, and waved to him as she walked off. He didn't wave back.

North American girls are supposed to be beautiful, he said.

Have you seen any?

What do you call her? He reached down for a tissue and sneezed out a double-barrel of snot. All of us had headaches and colds and coughs even with the heat cranked up, winter was kicking our asses. I had to wear a Christmas hat around the apartment to keep my shaven head warm; I looked like an unhappy tropical elf.

I wiped my nose. If this is the United States, mail me home.

Don't worry, Mami says. We're probably going home.

How does she know?

Her and Papi have been talking about it. She thinks it would be better if we went back. Rafa ran a finger glumly over our window; he didn't want to go; he liked the TV and the toilet and already saw himself with the girl in apartment four.

I don't know about that, I said. Papi doesn't look like he's going anywhere.

What do you know? You're just a little mojón.

I know more than you, I said. Papi had never once mentioned going back to the Island. I waited to get him in a good mood, after he had watched *Abbott and Costello*, and asked him if he thought we would be going back soon.

For what?

A visit.

Maybe, he grunted. Maybe not. Don't plan on it.

138

By the third week I was worried we weren't going to make it. Mami, who had been our authority on the Island, was dwindling. She cooked our food, and then sat there, waiting to wash the dishes. She had no friends, no neighbours to visit. You should talk to me, she said, but we told her to wait for Papi to get home. He'll talk to you, I guaranteed. Rafa's temper, which was sometimes a problem, got worse. I would tug at his hair, an old game of ours, and he would explode. We fought and fought and fought and after my mother pried us apart, instead of making up like the old days, we sat scowling on opposite sides of our room and planned each other's demise. I'm going to burn you alive, he promised. You should number your limbs, carbrón, I told him, so they'll know how to put you back together for the funeral. We squirted acid at each other with our eyes, like reptiles. Our boredom made everything worse.

One day I saw the brother and sister from apartment four gearing up to go play, and instead of waving I pulled on my parka. Rafa was sitting on the couch, flipping between a Chinese cooking show and an all-star Little League game. I'm going out, I told him.

Sure you are, he said, but when I pushed open the front door, he said, Hey!

The air outside was very cold and I nearly fell down our steps. No one in the neighbourhood was the shovelling type. Throwing my scarf over my mouth, I stumbled across the uneven crust of snow. I caught up to the brother and sister on the side of our building.

Wait up! I yelled. I want to play with you.

The brother watched me with a half grin, not understanding a word I'd said, his arms scrunched nervously at this side. His hair was a frightening no-colour. His sister had the greenest eyes and her freckled face was cowled in a hook of pink fur. We had on the same brand of mittens, brought cheap from Two Guys. I stopped and we faced each other, our white breath nearly reaching across the distance between us. The world was ice and the ice burned with sunlight. This was the first real encounter with North Americans and I felt loose and capable on that plain of ice. I motioned with my mittens and smiled. The sister turned to her brother and laughed. He said something to her and then she ran to where the other children were, the peals of her laughter trailing over her shoulder like spumes of her hot breath.

I've been meaning to come out, I said. But my father won't let us right now. He thinks we're too young, but look, I'm older than your sister, and my brother looks older than you.

The brother pointed at himself. Eric, he said.

My name's Joaquín, I said.

Juan, he said.

No, Joaquín, I repeated. Don't they teach you guys how to speak?

His grin never faded. Turning, he walked over to the approaching group of children. I knew that Rafa was watching me from the window and fought the urge to turn around and wave. The gringo children watched me from a distance and then walked away. Wait, I said, but then an Oldsmobile pulled into the next lot, its tires muddy and thick with snow. I couldn't follow them. The sister looked back once, a lick of her hair peeking out of her hood. After they had gone, I stood in the snow until my feet were cold. I was too afraid of getting my ass beat to go any farther.

Was it fun? Rafa was sprawled in front of the TV.

Hijo de la gran puta, I said, sitting down.

You look frozen.

I didn't answer him. We watched TV until a snowball struck the glass patio door and both of us jumped.

What was that? Mami wanted to know from her room.

Two more snowballs exploded on the glass. I peeked behind the curtain and saw the brother and the sister hiding behind a snow-buried Dodge.

Nothing, Señora, Rafa said. It's just snow.

What, is it learning how to dance out there?

It's just falling, Rafa said.

We both stood behind the curtain, and watched the brother throw fast and hard, like a pitcher.

Each day the trucks would roll into our neighbourhood with the garbage. The landfill stood two miles out, but the mechanics of the winter air conducted its sound and smells to us undiluted.

When we opened a window we could hear the bulldozers spreading the garbage out in thick, putrid layers across the top of the landfill. We could see the gulls attending the mound, thousands of them, wheeling.

Do you think kids play out there? I asked Rafa. We were standing on the porch, brave; at any moment Papi could pull into the parking lot and see us.

Of course they do. Wouldn't you?

I licked my lips. They must find a lot of crap out there.

Plenty, Rafa said.

That night I dreamed of home, that we'd never left. I woke up, my throat aching, hot with fever. I washed my face in the sink, then sat next to our window, my brother snoring, and watched the pebbles of ice falling and freezing into a shell over the cars and the snow and the pavement. Learning to sleep in new places was an ability you were supposed to lose as you grew older, but I never had it. The building was only now settling into itself; the tight magic of the just-hammered-in-nail was finally relaxing. I heard someone walking around in the living room and when I went out I found my mother standing in front of the patio door.

You can't sleep? she asked, her face smooth and perfect in the glare of the halogens.

I shook my head.

We've always been alike that way, she said. That won't make your life any easier.

I put my arms around her waist. That morning alone we'd seen three moving trucks from our patio door. I'm going to pray for Dominicans, she had said, her face against the glass, but what we would end up getting were Puerto Ricans.

She must have put me to bed because the next day I woke up next to Rafa. He was snoring. Papi was in the next room snoring as well, and something inside of me told me that I wasn't a quiet sleeper.

At the end of the month the bulldozers capped the landfill with a head of soft, blond dirt, and the evicted gulls flocked over with development, shitting and fussing, until the first of the new garbage was brought in.

My brother was bucking to be Number One Son: in all other things he was generally unchanged, but when it came to my father he listened with scrupulousness he had never afforded our mother. Papi said he wanted us inside, Rafa stayed inside. I was less attentive; I played in the snow for short stretches, though never out of sight of the apartment. You're going to get caught, Rafa forecasted. I could tell that my boldness made him miserable; from our windows he watched me packing snow and throwing myself into drifts. I stayed away from the gringos. When I saw the brother and sister from apartment four, I stopped farting around and watched for a sneak attack. Eric waved and his sister waved; I didn't wave back. Once he came over and showed me the baseball he must have just gotten. Roberto Clemente, he said, but I went on with building my fort. His sister grew flushed and said something loud and rude and then Eric sighed. Neither of them were handsome children.

One day the sister was out by herself and I followed her to the field. Huge concrete pipes sprawled here and there on the snow. She ducked into one of these and I followed her, crawling on my knees.

She sat in the pipes, crosslegged and grinning. She took her hands out of her mittens and rubbed them together. We were out of the wind and I followed her example. She poked a finger at me.

Joaquín, I said. All my friends call me Yunior.

Joaquín Yunior, she said. Elaine, Elaine Pitt.

Elaine.

Joaquín.

It's really cold, I said, my teeth chattering.

She said something and then felt the ends of my fingers. Cold, she said.

I knew that word already. I nodded. Frío. She showed me how to put my fingers in my armpits.

Warm, she said.

Yes, I said. Very warm.

At night, Mami and Papi talked. He sat on his side of the table and she leaned close, asking him, Do you ever plan on taking these children out? You can't keep them sealed up like this; they aren't dead yet.

They'll be going to school soon, he said, sucking on his pipe. And as soon as winter lets up I want to show you the ocean. You can see it around here you know, but it's better to see it up close.

How much longer does winter last?

Not long, he promised. You'll see. In a few months none of you will remember this and by then I won't have to work too much. We'll be able to travel in spring and see everything.

I hope so, Mami said.

My mother was not a woman easily cowed, but in the States she let my father roll over her. If he said he had to be at work for two days straight, she said okay and cooked enough moro to last him. She was depressed and sad and missed her father and her friends. Everyone had warned her that the U.S. was a difficult place where even the devil got his ass beat, but no one had told her that she would have to spend the rest of her natural life snow-bound with her children. She wrote letter after letter home, begging her sisters to come as soon as possible. I need the company, she explained. This neighbourhood is empty and friendless. And she begged Papi to bring his friends over. She wanted to talk about unimportant matters, and see a brown face who didn't call her mother or wife.

None of you are ready for guests, Papi said. Look at this house. Look at your children. Me dan vergüenza to see them slouching around like that.

You can't complain about this apartment. All I do is clean it.

What about your sons?

My mother looked over at me and then at Rafa. I put one shoe over the other. After that, she had Rafa keep after me about my shoelaces. When we heard the van arriving in the parking lot, Mami called us over for a quick inspection. Hair, teeth, hands feet. If anything was wrong she'd hide us in the bathroom until it was fixed. Her dinners grew elaborate. She even changed the TV for Papa without calling him a zángano.

Okay, he said finally. Maybe it can work.

It doesn't have to be that big a production, Mami said.

Two Fridays in a row he brought a friend over for dinner and Mami put on her best polyester jumpsuit and got us spiffy in our red pants, thick white belts, and amaranth-blue Chams shirts.

Seeing her asthmatic with excitement made us hopeful that our world was about to be transformed, but these were awkward dinners. The men were bachelors and divided their time between talking to Papi and eyeing Mami's ass. Papi seemed to enjoy their company but Mami spent her time on her feet, hustling food to the table, opening beers, and changing the channel. She started out each night natural and unreserved, with a face that scowled as easily as it grinned, but as the men loosened their belts and aired out their toes and talked their talk, she withdrew; her expressions narrowed until all that remained was a tight, guarded smile that seemed to drift across the room the way a splash of sunlight glides across a wall. We kids were ignored for the most part, except once, when the first man, Miguel, asked, Can you two box as well as your father?

They're fine fighters, Papi said.

You father is very fast. Has good hand speed. Miguel shook his head, laughing. I saw him finish this one tipo. He put fulano on his ass.

That *was* funny, Papi agreed. Miguel had brought a bottle of Bermúdez rum; he and Papi were drunk.

It's time you go to your room, Mami said, touching my shoulder.

Why? I asked. All we do is sit there.

That's how I feel about my home, Miguel said.

Mami's glare cut me in half. Such a fresh mouth, she said, showing us toward our room. We sat, as predicted, and listened.

On both visits, the men ate their fill, congratulated Mami on her cooking, Papi on his sons, and then stayed about an hour for propriety's sake. Cigarettes, dominos, gossip, and then the inevitable, Well, I have to get going. We have work tomorrow. You know how that is.

Of course I do. What else do we Dominicans know?

Afterward, Mami cleaned the pans quietly in the kitchen, scraping at the roasted pig flesh, while Papi sat out on our front porch in his short sleeves; he seemed to have grown impervious to the cold these last five years. When he came inside, he showered and pulled on his overalls. I have to work tonight, he said.

Mami stopped scratching at the pans with a spoon. You should find yourself a more regular job.

144

Papi smiled. Maybe I will.

As soon as he left, Mami ripped the needle from the album and interrupted Felix de Rosario. We heard her in the closet, pulling on her coat and her boots.

Do you think she's leaving us? I asked.

Rafa wrinkled his brow. It's a possibility, he said. What would you do if you were her?

I'd already be in Santo Dominigo.

When we heard the front door open, we let ourselves out of our room and found the apartment empty.

We better go after her, I said.

Rafa stopped at the door. Let's give her a minute, he said.

What's wrong with you? She's probably face down in the snow.

We'll wait two minutes, he said.

Shall I count?

Don't be a wiseguy.

One, I said loudly. He pressed his face against the glass patio door. We were about to hit the door when she returned, panting, an envelope of cold around her.

Where did you get to? I asked.

I went for a walk. She dropped her coat at the door; her face wasted from the cold and she was breathing deeply, as if she'd sprinted the last thirty steps.

Where?

Just around the corner.

Why the hell did you do that?

She started to cry, and when Rafa put his hand on her waist, she slapped it away. We went back to our room.

I think she's losing it, I said.

She's just lonely, Rafa said.

The night before the snowstorm I heard the wind at our window. I woke up the next morning, freezing. Mami was fiddling with the thermostat; we could hear the gurgle of water in the pipes but the apartment didn't get much warmer.

Just go play, Mami said. That will keep your mind off it.

Is it broken?

I don't know. She looked at the knob dubiously. Maybe it's slow this morning.

None of the gringos were outside playing. We sat by the window and waited for them. In the afternoon my father called from work; I could hear the forklifts when I answered.

Rafa?

No, it's me.

Get your mother.

How are you doing?

Get your mother.

We got a big storm on the way, he explained to her – even from where I was standing I could hear his voice. There's no way I can get out to see you. It's gonna be bad. Maybe I'll get there tomorrow.

What should I do?

Just keep indoors. And fill the tub with water.

Where are you sleeping? Mami asked.

At a friend's.

She turned her face from us. Okay, she said. When she got off the phone she sat in front of the TV. She could see I was going to pester her about Papi; she told me, Just watch the TV.

Radio WADO recommended spare blankets, water, flashlights, and food. We had none of these things. What happens if we get buried? I asked. Will we die? Will they have to save us in boats?

I don't know, Rafa said. I don't know anything about snow. I was spooking him. He went over to the window and peeked out.

We'll be fine, Mami said. As long as we're warm. She went over and raised the heat again.

But what if we get buried?

You can't have that much snow.

How do you know?

Because twelve inches isn't going to bury anybody, even a pain-in-the-ass like you.

I went out on the porch and watched the first snow begin to fall like finely-sifted ash. If we die, Papi's going to feel bad, I said.

Don't talk about it like that, Rafa said.

Mami turned away and laughed.

Four inches fell in an hour and the snow kept falling.

Mami waited until we were in bed, but I heard the door and woke Rafa. She's at it again, I said.

Outside?

You know it.

He put on his boots grimly. He paused at the door and then looked back at the empty apartment. Let's go, he said.

She was standing on the edge of the parking lot, ready to cross Westminister. The apartment lamps glared on the frozen ground and our breath was white in the night air. The snow was gusting.

Go home, she said.

We didn't move.

Did you at least lock the front door? she asked.

Rafa shook his head.

It's too cold for thieves anyway, I said.

Mami smiled and nearly slipped on the sidewalk. I'm not good at walking on this vaina.

I'm real good, I said. Just hold onto me.

We crossed Westminister. The cars were moving very slowly and the wind was loud and full of snow.

This isn't too bad, I said. These people should see a hurricane.

Where should we go? Rafa asked. He was blinking a lot to keep the snow out of his eyes.

Go straight, Mami said. That way we don't get lost.

We should mark the ice.

She put her hands around us both. It's easier if we go straight.

We went down to the edge of the apartments and looked out over the landfill, a misshapen, shadowy mound that abutted the Raritan. Rubbish fires burned all over it like sores and the dump trucks and bulldozers slept quietly and reverently at its base. It smelled like something the river had tossed out from its floor, something moist and heaving. We found the basketball courts next and the pool, empty of water, and Parkridge, the next neighbourhood over, which was full and had many, many children. We even saw the ocean, up there at the top of Westminister, like the blade of a long, curved knife. Mami was crying but we pretended not to notice. We threw snowballs at the sliding cars and once I removed my cap just to feel the snowflakes scatter across my cold, hard scalp.

CONTRIBUTORS

Naomi Alderman grew up in London and attended Oxford University and UEA. Her first novel, *Disobedience*, was published in 2006 in ten languages; it was read on BBC radio's Book at Bedtime and won the Orange Award for New Writers. Penguin published her second novel, *The Lessons* in April 2010. In 2007, she was named Sunday Times Young Writer of the Year, and one of Waterstones' 25 Writers for the Future. In 2009 she was shortlisted for the BBC National Short Story Award. From 2004 to 2007 Naomi was lead writer on the BAFTA-shortlisted alternate reality game Perplex City. She broadcasts regularly, and writes a weekly games column for the *Guardian*.

Niki Aguirre is an American fiction writer based in London. She has lived in the US, Spain and Ecuador and now resides in the UK. She studied English Literature at the University of Illinois and holds an MA in Creative Writing from the University of London. She is the recipient of a Birkbeck Outstanding Achievement Award for Fiction (2006). Her stories have appeared in various anthologies and publications including: *Tell Tales*, *LITRO*, and *Pen International Magazine*. Her debut collection of short fiction, *29 Ways to Drown*, was published in 2007 by flipped eye and was long-listed for the Frank O'Connor Award. Her second collection of short stories *Terminal Romance* is due out in 2011.

Tahmima Anam was born in Dhaka, Bangladesh in 1975. She was raised in Paris, New York City, and Bangkok. After studying at Mount Holyoke College and Harvard University, she earned a PhD in Social Anthropology. Her first novel, *A Golden Age*, was shortlisted for the Guardian First Book Award and the Costa First Novel Prize, and was the winner of the 2008 Commonwealth Writers Prize for Best First Book. It was translated into 22 languages. Her second novel, *The Good Muslim* came out in 2011. Her writing has been published in *Granta*, *The New York Times*, and the *Guardian*. She lives in London.

Brian Chikwava was born in Zimbabwe, which he left in 2002. His short story *Seventh Street Alchemy* was awarded the 2004 Caine Prize for African Writing and Chikwava became the first Zimbabwean to do so. His first novel, *Harare North*, was published in 2009. He has been a Charles Pick fellow at the University of East Anglia, and lives in London. He continues to write in England.

Junot Díaz was born in the Dominican Republic and raised in New Jersey. He is the author of *Drown* and *The Brief Wondrous Life of Oscar Wao*, which won the John Sargent, Sr., First Novel Prize; the National Book Critics Circle Award; the Anisfield-Wolf Book Award; and the 2008 Pulitzer Prize. Díaz has been awarded the Eugene McDermott Award, a fellowship from the Guggenheim Foundation, a Lila Acheson Wallace Reader's Digest Award, the 2002 PEN/Malamud Award, the 2003 U.S./Japan Creative Artist Fellowship from the National Endowment for the Arts, a fellowship at the Radcliffe Institute for Advanced Study at Harvard University, and the Rome Prize from the American Academy of Arts and Letters. He is the fiction editor at the *Boston Review* and the *Rudge (1948)*, and Nancy Allen Professor at the Massachusetts Institute of Technology. He lives in Cambridge, Massachusetts.

Romesh Gunesekera's *Reef* was shortlisted for the 1994 Booker Prize. He is also the author of *The Sandglass,* and *Heaven's Edge* which like his collection of stories, *Monkfish Moon,* was a New York Times Notable Book of the Year. His most recent novel is *The Match* (Bloomsbury). He was born in Sri Lanka and lives in London. He is a Fellow of the Royal Society of Literature and his poetry has been anthologized in Britain and the US.

Aamer Hussein was born in Karachi, Pakistan, in 1955, and moved to London in 1970. He is the author of five collections of short stories: *Mirror to the Sun* (1993), *This Other Salt* (1999), *Turquoise* (2002), *Cactus Town: Selected Stories* (2003) and *Insomnia* (2007). He is also the editor of *Kahani: Short Stories by Pakistani women* (2005). *Another Gulmohar Tree* (2009), and *The Cloud Messenger*.

Nam Le [www.namleonline.com] was born in Vietnam and raised in Australia. His first book, *The Boat*, won over a dozen major prizes, including the Australian Prime Minister's Literary Award, the Anisfield-Wolf Book Award, the Dylan Thomas Prize, the Melbourne Prize for Literature, and a U.S. National Book Foundation "5 Under 35" Fiction Award. *The Boat* was selected as a *New York Times* Notable Book and Editor's Choice, the best debut of 2008 by *New York Magazine*, the #1 book of 2008 by *The Oregonian,* and a book of the year by over thirty other venues around the world. Le is the fiction editor of the *Harvard Review*. He divides his time between Australia and abroad.

Monica Arac de Nyeko is from Uganda. She was shortlisted for the Caine Prize for African writing in 2004 for her story 'Strange Fruit', winning the prize in 2007 for 'Jambula Tree'. She is working on a novel.

Zoë Wicomb is a South African writer who lives in Glasgow where she is Emeritus Professor in the Department of English Studies at the University of Strathclyde. Her latest work of fiction is *The One That Got Away*; her critical work is on Postcolonial writing. Wicomb's short fiction can be found in various anthologies and journals, including the *Penguin Book of Contemporary South African Short Stories* and the *Heinemann Book of South African Short Stories*.

Nii Ayikwei Parkes is an author and performance poet. He is the author of the poetry chapbooks: *eyes of a boy, lips of a man* (1999), *M is for Madrigal* (2004), a selection of seven jazz poems and *Ballast* (2009), and his first full collection, *The Makings of You* (Peepal Tree, 2010). His novel, *Tail of the Blue Bird* was published by Jonathan Cape in 2009. Nii is the Senior Editor at flipped eye publishing, a contributing editor to *The Liberal*, a former poet in residence at The Poetry Café, a 2005 associate writer in residence on BBC Radio 3, and has held visiting positions at the University of Southampton and California State University.

OTHER ANTHOLOGIES FROM PEEPAL TREE

Tell-Tales 4: The Global Village
Edited by Courttia Newland and Monique Roffey
ISBN: 9781845230791; pp. 212; pub. 2009; price: £8.99

Tell Tales 4 is a groundbreaking collection of short stories from the UK-based Tell-Tales literary collective. Taking as its theme, The Global Village, this collection unites writers from around the world. Set in India, Africa, Jamaica, Trinidad, New York, London, cyberspace and the future, the stories are ambitious and very contemporary. Love, sex, death, war, global warming, immigration and crime are just some of the topics treated in often dark and funny ways. We are introduced to drug smugglers, a call-centre workers, tourists, ghosts and even a talking robot. The stories bring together exciting new talents and the work of established writers such as Caribbean luminary Olive Senior, well-known UK-based authors such as Matt Thorne, Sophie Woolley and Adam Thorpe; award-winning travel writer Justin Hill, hip hop journalist Michael Gonzales and Next Gen poet and short story writer Catherine Smith.

Red: Contemporary Black British Poetry
Edited by Kwame Dawes
ISBN: 9781845231293; pp. 252; pub. 2010; price: £9.99

Featuring Jackie Kay, Patience Agbabi, Nii Ayikwei Parkes, Raman Mundair, Maya Chowdhry, Dorothea Smartt, Fred D'Aguiar, Linton Kwesi Johnson, Bernardine Evaristo, John Lyons, Lemn Sissay, Grace Nichols, Jack Mapanje, Daljit Nagra, John Agard, Gemma Weekes and many more, *Red* collects poems by Black British poets writing with the word "red" in mind – as a kind of leap-off point, a context, a germ. It offers the reader the freedom to come to whatever conclusions they want to about what writing as a poet who is also Black and British might mean.

In this sense, *Red* is a different kind of anthology of Black British writing, and the richness of the entries, the moods, the humour, the passion, the reflection, the confessional all confirm that Black British poetry is a lively and defining force in Britain today.

Peepal Tree Press publishes Black British and Caribbean fiction, poetry, memoir and academic titles. It is the foremost publisher of Caribbean writing and has over 280 titles in print.

All Peepal Tree titles are available from the website
www.peepaltreepress.com
with a money back guarantee, secure credit card ordering and fast delivery throughout the world at cost or less.

Contact us at:
Peepal Tree Press, 17 King's Avenue, Leeds LS6 1QS, UK
Tel: +44 (0) 113 2451703
E-mail: contact@peepaltreepress.com